Come Home to Little House
Five Generations of Pioneer Girls

WHERE LITTLE HOUSE BEGAN

Martha Morse
Laura's great-grandmother
born 1782

BOSTON'S LITTLE HOUSE GIRL

Charlotte Tucker
Laura's grandmother
born 1809

SPIRIT OF THE WESTERN FRONTIER

Caroline Quiner
Laura's mother
born 1839

AMERICA'S ORIGINAL PIONEER GIRL

Laura Ingalls
born 1867

PIONEER FOR A NEW CENTURY

Rose Wilder
Laura's daughter
born 1886

Martha
(1782–1862) ——— Lewis Tucker

Lewis
(b. 1802)

Lydia
(b. 1805)

Thomas
(b. 1807)

Charlotte
(1809–1884)

Joseph
(1834–1862)

Henry
(1835–1882)

Martha
(1837–1927)

Mary
(1865–1928)

Laura
(1867–1957)

Family Tree ∽

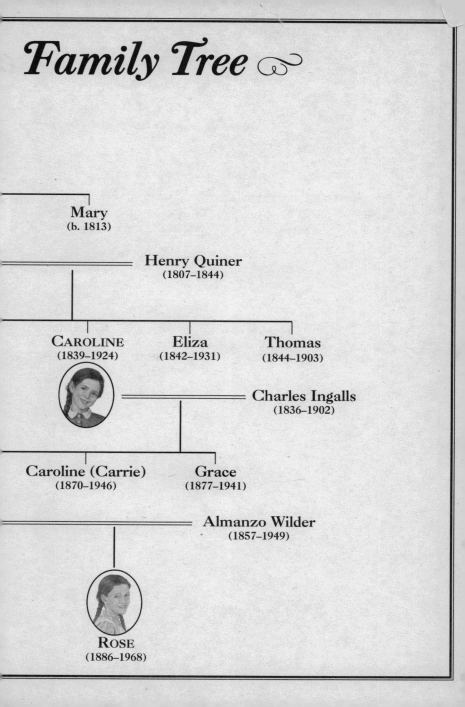

Mary
(b. 1813)

Henry Quiner
(1807–1844)

CAROLINE
(1839–1924)

Eliza
(1842–1931)

Thomas
(1844–1903)

Charles Ingalls
(1836–1902)

Caroline (Carrie)
(1870–1946)

Grace
(1877–1941)

Almanzo Wilder
(1857–1949)

ROSE
(1886–1968)

Across *the* Rolling River

Celia Wilkins

Illustrations by Dan Andreasen

HarperTrophy®
An Imprint of HarperCollinsPublishers

*For help in researching this book, the author would like to thank
William F. Jannke III, Amy Edgar Sklansky, Theresa Peterson,
Travis Coomer, Eben and Charlotte Henson, and Maria Janzow.
For input and help along the way, many thanks to Lissa Peterson,
Kara Vicinelli, Tara Weikum, and Tim Ungs. For guidance and
understanding, deepest gratitude to my editor, Alix Reid.*

Harper Trophy®, ▩®, Little House®, and The Caroline Years™
are trademarks of HarperCollins Publishers Inc.

Library of Congress Cataloging-in-Publication Data
Wilkins, Celia.
  Across the rolling river / Celia Wilkins ; illustrations by Dan
Andreasen.
      p.   cm.
  Summary: Follows the experiences of Caroline Quiner, who will
become Laura Ingalls Wilder's mother, and her family on their farm on
the Wisconsin frontier during the year in which Caroline turns twelve.
  ISBN 0-06-027004-7 — ISBN 0-06-027005-5 (lib. bdg.)
  ISBN 0-06-440734-9 (pbk.)
  1. Ingalls, Caroline Lake Quiner—Juvenile fiction.   [1. Ingalls,
Caroline Lake Quiner—Fiction.   2. Wilder, Laura Ingalls, 1867–1957—
Family—Fiction.   Frontier and pioneer life—Wisconsin—Fiction.
4. Wisconsin—Fiction.]   I. Title.   II. Series: Little House.
III. Andreasen, Dan, ill.
PZ7.W648498 Ac   2001   2001024397
[Fic]—dc21   CIP
                                                            AC

3   4   5   6   7   8   9   10

❖

First Harper Trophy edition, 2001

Author's Note

Many years before she ever put pen to paper to create what would become the Little House books, Laura Ingalls Wilder wrote to her aunt Martha Quiner Carpenter and asked her to "tell the story of those days" when she and Laura's mother, Caroline, were young girls. Laura's mother had never talked much about her childhood in the newly settled Wisconsin territory, and so Aunt Martha wrote several letters to Laura filled with memories of the Quiners' day-to-day life during the 1840s and 1850s. These letters became the basis for the Caroline series.

Through the letters and through careful research, I came to understand that times were not always easy for young Caroline and her family. There were years of hardship after the sudden, tragic death of Caroline's father—years in which Caroline learned firsthand what it took to survive in a vast and sometimes unforgiving wilderness. It took courage and resilience and an indomitable pioneer spirit— the very traits Caroline would pass on to her own daughters after she had grown up and married another child of the western frontier, Charles Ingalls.

In Across the Rolling River *I have sought to present the most realistic portrait possible of Caroline Quiner's life, while trying to stay true to Laura's own depiction of her beloved Ma in the Little House books.*

—C.W.

Contents

Across *the* Rolling River

A Voice in the Woods

The sky between the tall fir trees glowed rosy purple as Caroline Quiner followed her brother Henry through the late-afternoon woods. It was the first of September, and the air was still heavy with summer. The leaves had not begun to burn with fall color, and the forest floor was still a lush and mossy green. The songbirds had come out to sing their final songs before the night closed in.

Fear not, fear not! called the red-breasted robins, darting in pairs among the tall grasses.

And Caroline was not the least bit fearful, even though the shadows were already growing thick in places along the path to the river. She had lived in these woods for nearly three years now, ever since Mother had moved the family west from Brookfield to the little farm in the middle of a vast stretch of Wisconsin wilderness.

Back then the farm was hardly a farm at all. It was a tiny clearing surrounded by towering firs and pines and oaks, wild cherry and hickory. There had been no garden, no fields of corn and wheat, oats and barley. There had been no barn and no animals to keep. There had been no wood-frame house with an upstairs and a downstairs, a room for the girls and a room for the boys, a large kitchen, and even a parlor. There had been only a rough two-room log cabin in which Caroline and her five brothers and sisters had lived with Mother, and later with their new pa, who had married Mother five years after Caroline's own father had been lost when his trading ship went down in a terrible storm.

All these things—the prospering fields, the barn, the wonderful new house—had come after hard work. So much hard work, Caroline could still feel the way her whole body had ached morning, noon, and night from helping to clear the land and sow the crops and bring in the harvest before a first frost could leave the family in debt and starving for winter.

Not that the hard work was over. Far from it. Henry liked to say that being a farmer was just like signing up for a lifetime of thankless labor. But at least things were not quite so difficult as they had been three years before.

"Wheat is king!" all the newspapers from Milwaukee to Madison had been shouting. And the almanac had said 1851 would be a good year—not too wet and not too dry. So Pa, who had been Mr. Holbrook before he married Mother, had traded lumber for Slow and Ready, a pair of good strong oxen. Once the wheat was cut, it would be hauled to the mill, where the miller would grind it into flour. Some of the flour Caroline's family would keep, but Pa was hoping to sell some to the miller for a good profit.

Now the wheat was sitting ripe in the fields, just waiting to be cut. But today there was no cutting—no work at all, in fact, except of course for the chores that must be done no matter what. It was Sunday, the day of rest. In the morning Pa had hitched Slow and Ready to the wagon, and the family had ridden the three miles to the growing town of Concord to attend church. In the afternoon they had all sat in the parlor while Mother read to them from the Bible. It was nice to rest, but it was hard to sit still all day long—even though Caroline was nearly twelve years old, and old enough not to wriggle like nine-year-old Eliza and seven-year-old Thomas. Martha hardly ever wriggled anymore. She was fourteen and had begun to wear her skirts longer and her brown hair pinned up. Joseph never wriggled either. He was very nearly a grown man—seventeen years old. Henry was only a year younger than Joseph, but it was clear he would never stop wriggling. Caroline knew it took all his will-power to sit quietly on Sunday afternoons. He was always itching to move.

He was moving now, darting in and out among the trees ahead of Caroline, their dog Wolf at his heels. They were on their way to the river to fetch Baby and Bess, the milk cow and her calf. All day long, even on Sunday, the animals roamed free to graze the land. It was Henry's job to round them up and bring them back to the barn before nightfall. Sometimes, if Caroline finished seeing to the hens and geese in time, she went with Henry to find Baby and Bess at their favorite marshy places along the river's edge.

"C'mon, Caroline," Henry called over his shoulder. "Race you to the river."

Caroline shook her head. "You mustn't race on a Sunday. And besides, ladies don't race at all."

Henry stopped in his tracks and gave a loud snort. "Aw, you're not a lady. Not yet any-ways," he said with his familiar lopsided grin. "Seems to me you'd want to run as much as you can before you turn as funny as Martha."

Caroline let out a little sigh. It was true that

Martha had been acting funny for a while now. At first Caroline could not stand the way Martha tried to be so grown-up all the time. But lately she had started to understand Martha a little better. Caroline often felt torn inside. Some days she wished she could still play with dolls like Eliza, but some days she had no patience for childish games and wished she could wear her hair up like Martha.

"Boys can whistle, but girls must sing," Caroline replied. It was something Mother said occasionally. It meant that boys could be boys, but girls must be quiet and sweet and do lady-like things.

"I wouldn't mind only singing if I could sound like that thrush," Henry said, cocking his head up toward the treetops.

Caroline followed Henry's gaze. She couldn't see the bird, but she knew it was a thrush. The small brown bird always came out before sundown and perched in the highest branches. Its song was so lively and clear, it made all the other birds sound almost dull and ordinary.

The bird paused for a moment in its song

as if to catch its breath, and all of a sudden another sound came out slow and soft from somewhere deeper in the woods. It was the strangest sound Caroline had ever heard. At first it seemed to mimic the thrush's song, just as a mockingbird could do, but its notes were not quite so high. It throbbed faintly, starting out low and building in a rush. It was an eerie, unearthly sound, as if the trees themselves were singing.

Wolf's ears were up, and he let out a low growl deep in his throat.

"Hush," Henry said, but he gave Caroline a puzzled, wide-eyed stare. They all stood for several minutes, listening. Abruptly the sound stopped and the thrush began to sing, louder and bolder, as if to say, "I am the king of the forest." But after a while the little bird paused once more, and the other voice started up again, rising higher and higher. The sound was part cry, part song. It made the hair on the back of Caroline's neck stand on end. She thought about turning around and heading back to the house to find Pa, but something was drawing her forward as well. Henry and Wolf began to make their way on quiet feet toward the sound, and Caroline followed.

The strange voice grew louder. Caroline thought that Wolf would begin to growl again, but he did not. He whined a little, and his tail wagged once and then was still. His ears went back down, and he sniffed the air. He was gazing at something through the trees, and Caroline peered around the trunk of a fat oak to see what had caught his attention.

A boy was standing in a clearing near the river's edge. He was working at something that glinted bright in the last rays of sunlight, and all at once Caroline saw that the voice was a fiddle. The strange boy was playing a honey-colored fiddle. The long bow zigzagged over the strings. The sound was not so eerie now. It was bright and cheerful, echoing the thrush's merry song. Back and forth the voices went, as if in dialogue with each other. Sometimes they merged as if singing a duet.

Finally the boy seemed to sense that he was not alone. He turned and, catching sight of

Caroline peeking at him, continued to play. He raised one eyebrow and grinned a friendly grin as he dipped and bowed, his whole body moving in time to the rhythm. The sound made Caroline want to clap and dance and stand still and listen all at once. She had heard fiddle players before, but only when they had played familiar tunes. This sound was so completely unfamiliar, it seemed to be the voice of the woods itself.

Suddenly the music stopped. The boy put down his fiddle. The thrush's song went on, and everything went back to normal. Henry stepped forward and loudly clapped his hands. Wolf growled a little but then busied himself with sniffing at the brush along the river. The boy gave a low bow.

"That was some fine playing," Henry said. "Where'd you learn to fiddle like that?"

The boy shrugged. "Picked it up here and there," he replied.

Caroline came out from behind the oak tree and stood beside her brother. The boy was a little taller than Henry but looked to be about the same age. He wore dark trousers rolled up nearly to his knees and a clean gray-linen workshirt under red suspenders. His feet were bare, and his short hair was dark brown and very thick. It stood straight up in tufts here and there, as if he had been running his hands through it. His eyes were of the deepest blue, and they seemed to laugh at some secret joke. When he grinned his friendly grin, Caroline suddenly felt like laughing even though there was nothing to laugh at.

"What are you doing way out here playing with the birds?" Henry asked.

"A body can learn a lot from listening to nature," the boy said. "Besides, my pa won't let me play on a Sunday. But I took a notion to sneak my fiddle along while I rounded up the cows."

"That's what we're doing too," Henry said. "Rounding up the cows."

The boy raised his chin. "Saw a fawn-colored cow and a spotted heifer downriver a piece."

"That'd be our Baby and Bess," Henry said,

looking off toward the woods and then back again. "Where are you from, anyway? This here is my pa's land, and I've never seen you before."

"Beg your pardon for trespassing, but we only just arrived," the boy said. "We come from back east."

"Yorkers?" Henry asked, and when the boy answered yes, Henry nodded knowingly. The woods were filling up with people from New York, and folks had started calling them Yorkers. Sometimes it seemed as if the whole state of New York was moving to Wisconsin. Pa said it was because land offices in the east were full of advertisements proclaiming Wisconsin to be a settlers' dream. Rich land at cheap prices.

"Come by boat?" Henry asked. Caroline knew that most of the Yorkers came through the Erie Canal on mule boats and then down the Great Lakes. It took only a couple of weeks to travel all the way from Buffalo to Milwaukee.

But the boy was shaking his head. "I've

been riding in a wagon since I was knee high to a grasshopper. We stopped in Illinois for a time, but Pa took a notion to try our luck here. He bought up some land just on the other side of the river." He pointed out across the water.

"We're neighbors then," Henry said. "I'm Henry Quiner, and this is my sister Caroline."

The boy shifted his fiddle to one side and shook hands with Henry. He then gave a little bow, touching his finger to his brow as if tipping a hat to Caroline.

"Pleased to meet you," he said.

Caroline suddenly felt shy under his clear blue gaze. She gave a quick smile and ducked her head.

"Anyhow, what are you doing over here?" Henry asked. "Your cows didn't cross the river, did they?"

"Naw," the boy answered. "They're just on the other side." He pointed with his bow. "I wanted to put a little space between me and home, so my folks couldn't hear me play. Then I followed the sound of that thrush. It seemed to want company singing."

They stood listening to the bird sing by himself for a time. Then Henry sighed and squinted up to the sky. "Well, we've got to get the cows home before the sun goes down," he said, and Caroline thought he sounded disappointed to be leaving their new acquaintance. Then he perked up. "Hey, Pa's planning on cutting our wheat tomorrow, as long as the dry weather holds. If you folks are looking to trade work, we'd be happy to have you, seeing as we're neighbors and all."

The boy looked thoughtful for a moment. "I'll let my pa know," he said before he gave a little wave and tucked his fiddle and bow under his arm. Caroline and Henry stood watching as he waded back across the river, which was running low after a long, hot summer. When he reached the far side, he turned and raised his fiddle in the air.

"Hey," Henry called. "What's your name, anyhow?"

"Ingalls," the boy called back across the rippling water. "Charlie Ingalls." He gave a final wave and disappeared into the woods.

"Playing with the birds," Henry said, shaking his head. "If that don't beat all."

Caroline and Henry began to walk in the direction Charlie Ingalls had pointed, and soon they heard the soft clanging of the cowbells. Baby and Bess looked up from their grazing, slowly blinking their large brown eyes. Wolf gave a short bark and nipped at their hooves, sending them trotting toward home.

As they walked between the trees, Caroline could still hear the thrush singing to himself. She thought about Charlie Ingalls and his fiddle playing until she reached the clearing, and then there were other things to think about. Henry settled down to do the milking, and Caroline hurried into the house to help with supper. Inside the large kitchen Martha and Eliza were already setting the table and talking of the new teacher.

"I hope she will be pretty and nice," Eliza said, smoothing down the skirt of her yellow gingham dress. Caroline knew she was wondering what the new teacher would wear. Eliza liked fine clothes just like Caroline.

"I hope she doesn't use the ruler like old Mr. Crenshaw," Martha said, scowling. Caroline knew that Martha did not like school as much as she did. Martha had often told Caroline that she would prefer to stay at home and help Mother rather than spend the day inside a schoolhouse.

Caroline was about to chime in with her own hopes about the new teacher when Mother came out of the pantry carrying the platter of cold roast chicken left over from dinner. The petticoats under her dark-blue calico skirt swished, and the heels of her black boots tapped briskly on the wide plank floor. Her black hair was parted in the middle and pulled smoothly back, and it shone in the lamplight. Her green eyes were smiling but serious. "I am quite sure you girls will never give the teacher reason to use the ruler," she said firmly.

Caroline exchanged quick, silent glances with her sisters. Last term it had seemed as if Mr. Crenshaw needed very little reason to use the ruler. Caroline did not like to think ill of anyone, but she had been convinced that Mr.

Crenshaw simply enjoyed the sound the ruler made as it rapped down upon the hands of some unlucky scholar. Even though she had never gone home with swollen knuckles, she was glad Mr. Crenshaw had not returned to teach another term.

"Besides," Mother continued, "no use wasting precious time wondering about our Miss May. We shall meet her soon enough, and we shall have plenty of time to become acquainted."

And that was true. The new teacher was set to arrive in two weeks' time. Not only that, but she would be living under the very same roof as Caroline and her sisters. Each term one family had to board the teacher, and this term Pa and Mother had agreed to do it.

For weeks Caroline and Martha and Eliza had been full of questions about "our Miss May," as they had begun to call her. Would she be fashionable? Would she be young? Would she be kind? Since she was coming from the east, Caroline thought she might be snooty and turn her nose up at everything around her.

The home Pa had built for them out of shining new planks cut and sanded at the mill was the largest and most beautiful house Caroline had ever lived in, but she knew there were far finer houses back east. Indeed, there were far finer houses only three miles away, in Concord. Mr. Kellogg, a special friend of the family's and the richest man in these parts, owned such a house. Its large rooms were filled with elegant store-bought furniture. The walls of its parlor were papered in a dainty flower print, and its hardwood floors were covered with thick woven rugs.

But as Caroline looked around the neat kitchen with its shining black iron stove, solid oak table and chairs, and handsome dish dresser, she decided that if their house was good enough for Mother, who had also come from back east, it was certainly good enough for the unknown Miss May.

"A red sky tonight." Pa's deep voice came from inside the lean-to as he stood at the china basin washing his hands. The lean-to was a little room with a slanted roof that was just outside the kitchen door. It held the woodpile and the china basin for washing up.

"Fair skies for tomorrow then," Joseph's voice added, for that was what the almanac always said. A red sky at sunset meant good weather the following day.

Pa's boots made a slight dragging sound as he walked through the kitchen door. Two years before, they had all been near death with cholera, except for Joseph and Thomas. By some miracle—and thanks to Grandma, who had come all the way from Milwaukee to nurse them—they had all recovered. But Pa had been left with a stiffening in his joints and a heaviness in one leg. It made him slower at going about the chores, but he never complained. He always said he was glad to have three strong boys to help him.

"Fair skies and a full harvest moon tomorrow night," Pa repeated to Mother. "We couldn't ask for a better time to cut the wheat. We'll have a mighty fine harvest, Charlotte."

"The good Lord willing, Frederick," Mother said quietly.

Pa's blue eyes smiled at Mother. "The good Lord willing," he replied, easing himself into his chair and placing his large hands flat on the table. Even sitting, Pa was a tall man. He wore his brown hair combed neatly back and tied with a string of rawhide. The bushy strip of beard framing his jaw was just beginning to show some gray.

Two years before, Caroline had not known whether she would like having a new pa. Back then she could think of him only as Mr. Holbrook, and he had seemed very stiff and unsmiling. Henry had not liked him at all, because he was such a hard taskmaster. But slowly things had changed. Pa and Henry had come to an understanding, and Pa's gruff ways had softened. Now Caroline could hardly imagine life without Pa. And she knew her brothers and sisters felt the same.

"Mighty fine-looking biscuits," Pa said now as Mother set them on the table.

Caroline smiled at the compliment. She had made the biscuits herself the day before. Saturday was always her favorite day because that was when they did the baking.

"Nothing like Caroline's biscuits," Joseph added as he took his place to the right of Pa. It was hard to believe, but Joseph was as tall as Pa now. His shoulders were broad and strong from clearing trees and plowing the land. Like Pa, he had a quiet manner. He always thought before he spoke, unlike his brothers.

"Henry's late with the milking!" Thomas almost shouted, bursting into the room.

"Now Thomas," Mother scolded. "Sunday is not a day to raise our voices except in prayer."

Thomas lowered his head so that his blond curls fell over his face. He quietly took his seat next to Joseph as Henry came rushing through the door with the milk pail.

Mother gave him a stern look. "I hope you didn't spill any in your hurry, young man," she said.

"No, ma'am," Henry answered, setting the pail carefully on the counter of the dish dresser. He went back out into the lean-to to wash up and then hurried to the table. It didn't matter whether it was breakfast, dinner, or supper, mealtime was always Henry's favorite time of the day.

Mother ladled the warm, frothy milk into the cups, and Eliza set them around at each plate. Mother poured the rest of the milk into shallow pans, and Caroline and Martha carried them into the pantry to sit overnight. Tomorrow morning they would skim the cream off the tops, and later that week they would make more butter to add to the supply in the root cellar.

When everyone was seated, Pa said the blessing and they ate the cold roasted chicken. Along with Caroline's biscuits there was butter and honey from the bee farm Thomas tended.

"Early to bed, early to rise," Mother said when they were finished. Caroline knew she was thinking of the long day ahead of them tomorrow. A full harvest moon meant extra hours of light. Pa and the boys would be working all day and into the night to get the wheat in, and Mother and the girls would be busy too, getting the food ready for all the workers.

Now that there were other families nearby, Pa and the boys were able to trade work. This meant the cutting would go more quickly, but it also meant more mouths to feed.

As soon as the dishes were wiped and put away, Caroline and Eliza followed Martha upstairs. A plank wall separated the girls' bedroom from the boys'. In the girls' room there was one large bed covered with the nine-patch quilt Martha and Caroline had made. A tall wardrobe sat against one wall and a chest of drawers sat against the other. One square window, with real glass windowpanes, looked out over the clearing.

After she had changed into her nightgown and put her dress away, Caroline stood brushing out her long brown hair, gazing out the window at the nighttime world. The moon was nearly full, and the clearing was bathed in a soft, pearly light.

"I heard the trees singing today," Caroline suddenly said, whispering it so that Mother would not hear. Caroline knew Mother would never approve of fiddle playing on a Sunday.

"Whatever do you mean?" Martha asked.

And so Caroline told all about the strange boy and how he had made his fiddle sound as if the trees had a voice of their own.

"Do you think he will come tomorrow?" Eliza asked.

"I don't know," Caroline replied.

"I hope he does," Eliza said after thinking about it for a moment.

As Caroline tucked her hair into her night-cap and got into bed beside her sisters, she realized that she too hoped that their new neighbor would make an appearance in the morning, and that he would bring along his honey-colored fiddle.

Many Hands

Before the sun had even risen, Caroline's eyes opened to the familiar sound of her brothers' loud voices in the room next door.

"Get to moving, Tommy," Joseph jokingly scolded. "You are a big boy now, and will need to look sharp today."

Thomas replied sleepily that he thought he might try his hand at cradling that day, but Joseph only laughed. "Plenty of time for that," he said, and Henry added, "Cradling makes the whole body ache. If I was you, I'd be glad to stay a water boy for another year yet."

Breakfast was eaten in a hurry so that the chores could be done before the helpers arrived. Quickly Caroline saw to the hens and geese and then returned to the kitchen to help Mother with the cooking. There would be chicken pies and baked beans and corn bread, and beets fresh from the garden. For dessert they had already baked a blueberry pie and a huckleberry pie. Caroline went to check on the pies where they sat under clean dish towels on their own shelf in the pantry.

The pantry had been Pa's special gift to Mother when he built the house. It was a little room off the kitchen to the left of the stove. Its walls were fitted with handy shelves and drawers and cupboards. Caroline never grew tired of looking at that pantry. It was like having their very own general store. The drawers held the biscuits and breads from Saturday's baking, and the upper shelves held the pies. There were cupboards for cornmeal and sugar and spices. Four large barrels sat on the floor, filled with flour, salt, molasses, and salt pork. The shelves along one wall held Mother's pots and pans and jars and crocks.

In the middle of the pantry floor Pa had built a trap door leading down into the root cellar where the butter and vegetables and preserves and herbs were stored.

"Please bring out some honey," Mother called, so Caroline reached up to the topmost shelf for a jar of honey. When she came back into the kitchen, there was already the sound of voices in the clearing. Caroline felt a little flutter of nervous excitement. It was nice to have families about to help, but Caroline was always shy at first with new faces.

"Mighty fine day," a man's voice called out. It was the widower Mr. Graylick, and his son, Jacob. They were Yorkers who had moved to Concord a few months before. They stood talking with Pa, leaning on the cradles they had brought in their wagon. A cradle was a special scythe that had been fitted with a framework of long wooden slats around its sharp steel blade. The blade cut the tall stalks of wheat, and the wooden frame caught the wheat and held it. Then the cradle could be swung so that the cut wheat was left in neat piles the length of the field.

Joseph and Henry went to the barn to bring out their own cradles as another wagon pulled up. The Wighams and the Spiveys had ridden together. Both families owned land just on the other side of the Territorial Road, which led into Concord.

Mr. Wigham and Mr. Spivey shouted out their greetings and headed to the field right away with their cradles, while their wives swept into the kitchen with their baskets of food.

Caroline watched as Mother greeted the ladies warmly. Mother never seemed shy or flustered around guests.

"So nice to see you," Mother said. "It was good of you all to come."

"'Many hands make light work.'" Mrs. Wigham gave the old saying in her cheerful voice. She was young and pretty, and had a brand-new baby named Daniel. She had

27

brought fried chicken and sweet potatoes and corn bread and dried-apple pie.

Mrs. Spivey had come with her daughter, Nell. They had brought smoked ham and biscuits and corn relish and graham bread and strawberry preserves. Caroline supposed Mrs. Spivey was Mother's age, but she seemed much older, with drab gray hair pulled back severely and a constant frown on her long, thin face.

Nell was a year older than Martha, and she was nothing like her mother. She was fair, with lovely blue eyes that always seemed to be smiling, especially, it seemed to Caroline, at Jacob Graylick.

The ladies bustled about the kitchen, getting the food ready for dinner, while Nell and Martha took care of the baby. Caroline and Eliza went to fetch some more water from the well. Only last year going to fetch water had meant walking all the way to the river. But now a well sat only a stone's throw from the kitchen door.

Thomas was already at the well, drawing a

bucket of cool water up with the long rope so he could fill the jugs for the men. Caroline and Eliza were waiting their turn when they heard a noise behind them. Caroline turned to see Charlie Ingalls and two other boys coming out of the woods. Wolf rushed forward, barking ferociously, but Caroline called out to him, and he stopped right away. Charlie Ingalls grinned and waved at Caroline. He was carrying a cradle and his fiddle box.

"Is that him?" Eliza whispered, and Caroline nodded.

"I guess the beast didn't recognize me without hearing me play," Charlie laughed, nodding at Wolf. Then he turned and introduced his brothers. "This is Peter, and this is Lansford James, though he's Jamie to us."

Peter stepped forward. He was several years older than Charlie, but he had the same dark hair and twinkling blue eyes. "Pa had to go to Watertown, and the baby is sickly, otherwise Ma and the girls would have come too," he explained, letting his cradle rest on the ground. "But Charlie told us that you'd be cutting today, and we're glad to help where we can."

Jamie was perhaps a year older than Thomas. He had light-brown hair and brown eyes. He did not carry a cradle, but he held out something wrapped in clean cloth. "Ma sent along this blackberry pie."

Caroline took the pie and smiled shyly at the three boys. "Thank you," she said, trying to sound as warm and sure of herself as Mother sounded when greeting guests.

Thomas asked why Charlie had brought a fiddle. "Do you mean to fiddle the wheat out of the field?"

"Wait and see," Charlie said, and he gave a wink that made Eliza giggle.

The boys went off to the field, and the girls went back into the kitchen with Mrs. Ingalls' blackberry pie and a bucket of water.

The women were talking about the new teacher.

"Coming all the way from Albany by herself!" Mrs. Wigham exclaimed. "She must be a brave soul."

"I've heard it's quite safe traveling along the

canals," Mother replied.

"Yes, but this is still such wild country," Mrs. Spivey said. "I would never have come here of my own accord, if Mr. Spivey had not taken it into his head to bring us."

Caroline glanced at Mother, wondering if she would say anything. Mother had traveled with Father from Boston to Ohio to Wisconsin before Caroline was born. But she had brought the family from Brookfield to this part of the country all by herself.

"We're lucky to have any teacher at all." Mrs. Wigham spoke up before Mother had a chance to resond to Mrs. Spivey's words. "As you know, my husband is on the school board, and it was not easy to find a replacement for Mr. Crenshaw. Not many teachers want to come into the wilderness to teach."

"She must be one of those modern young women we've been reading about in the newspapers." Mrs. Spivey sneered. "I wouldn't be surprised if she arrived in that awful bloomer costume."

"I hope she does!" Nell boldly said. "I

wouldn't mind wearing it myself."

"Nell!" Mrs. Spivey exclaimed. "You'll do no such thing as long as you live under my roof. The very idea of a lady parading around in trousers for all the world to see!"

Nell ducked her head, but when she looked sideways at Martha, Caroline saw her eyes flash defiantly. Caroline had read about bloomers in the magazine *Godey's Lady's Book*. Back east a woman named Amelia Bloomer had begun to wear silken trousers under shorter skirts. The new style had caused quite a stir. Some people applauded it, but others found it grotesque. Ladies wearing bloomers had been banned from churches and other public places. Lately there had been articles in the *Watertown Chronicle* announcing that bloomers had finally made their appearance in Wisconsin. When Caroline and Martha and Eliza had first read about them, Eliza had wanted to put on the boys' trousers under their skirts, but Caroline had insisted it was a silly notion. She knew that real bloomers were made from soft silk, and they were wide and flowing until they gathered at the ankle. Caroline thought she might have the courage to wear a new style if it were pretty enough, but she had no desire to put on her brothers' old trousers.

"*Godey's* maintains that the costume is quite comfortable and practical," Mrs. Wigham said. "What do you think, Charlotte?"

They all turned to Mother. Everyone knew that she had been a dressmaker back in Boston before she had married, and so her opinion would mean a great deal.

"I must admit I am not sure I approve of ladies wearing trousers," Mother answered slowly. "Though I've often thought that shorter skirts would be more practical, especially out here where there is so much mud to contend with."

Mrs. Spivey clucked her tongue. "I, for one, would not allow a daughter of mine to attend a school where the teacher wore bloomers."

Nell gave Martha another quick look that said, "We would have to see about that," but she did not utter a word out loud.

Mrs. Spivey continued, "And another thing: I do not know that a lady should be teaching at all. Especially out here in this country, where the boys grow up wild as bears. Everyone knows that female teachers have a harder time keeping order. Sometimes boys like running a teacher out of town just for fun."

"We have had no trouble so far," Mother said in her gentle voice.

"Mark my words," Mrs. Spivey replied harshly. "A rotten apple spoils the bunch."

The room was quiet for a time. All the laughter and chatter seemed to have been chased off by Mrs. Spivey's ill temper. Caroline thought that Mrs. Spivey was wrong. Lady teachers were just as capable as men teachers. And Caroline knew her brothers were not wild as bears even though they had been raised here. As Caroline watched Mrs. Spivey's sour face, she thought that truer words had never been spoken—a rotten apple did spoil the bunch.

Soon, though, Mrs. Wigham was chatting again in her cheerful way. She told them of the newly dug artesian well she had visited when staying with her sister-in-law in Watertown the month before.

"The water is quite refreshing," she said, "and it is reputed to heal anything that ails you." She turned to Mrs. Spivey. "Have you ever tried any?"

"No," Mrs. Spivey said, and her voice was cold.

Caroline thought they would be plunged into silence again, but Mother was quick to keep the conversation going. "I am very happy with our new minister," she said, and at last Mrs. Spivey had something to smile and be agreeable about. Caroline did not see how anyone could not like Reverend Longly. He had such a pleasant way of delivering his sermons. Mother and Mrs. Spivey and Mrs. Wigham talked of church matters until it was nearly noon.

"Time to set up the table." Mother said. "I'm sure the men will be hungry."

Earlier that morning Pa and the boys had placed long planks on blocks of wood to make a large table in the yard. Now Caroline and

Eliza smoothed two of Mother's pretty red-and-white-checkered tablecloths over the boards, and then helped set out all the platters and plates and bowls of food. When everything was ready, Mother took a serving spoon and banged it on an old tin pan.

A great yell rose up from the far end of the field. The men and boys dropped their cradles and stretched out their backs and came striding across the clearing. They washed their hands and faces in the buckets of water Thomas and Jamie had ready and took their places at the long table. Caroline helped the women dish out the food to the hungry workers. The girls and mothers would eat after the men had gone back to the field.

Pa's face was red from the sun, but he was smiling. He was pleased with the morning's work. There was not a cloud in the clear blue sky. With all these helpers the wheat would be cut in no time.

"It would go even quicker if we had one of those newfangled mechanical reapers." Mr. Spivey spoke up between mouthfuls.

"I've read about that fellow McCormick in the papers," Pa said, "but we haven't seen one of his machines out here yet."

"Back in New York we saw a few," Mr. Graylick said. "Farmers pull their money together so that everybody has a chance to use it for a time."

"Sound idea," Joseph responded, and Caroline glanced at his serious, thoughtful face as she helped serve up the chicken pie. Even though she knew Joseph was older now, it still made her wonder at how grown-up he had become.

"But I don't see how such a machine could get around all these stumps," Mr. Graylick said. "We have enough trouble with the cradles. Back on my farm in New York, the land was already flat and clean. Not a tree stump anywhere. That reaper went smooth right across a field. Twice as fast as any of us went today."

The men ate silently for a moment, thinking about that. Caroline glanced at the half-cut field. The wheat had been planted around the stumps of the trees that had been cut. The stumps would stay there for years, and for years Pa and the boys would be grubbing at them to make sure the little shoots poking up in the old wood would not grow into more trees. Pa said the stumps would eventually rot and be soft enough to pull up out of the earth with the help of the oxen.

"Hard to imagine a machine doing the work of a man," Joseph spoke up again.

"Not so hard for me to imagine," Henry replied, and everyone laughed.

"Young Henry would have machines to do all his chores if he could," Pa said, but he said it jokingly. There had been a time when Pa would never have teased Henry so easily, but now there was no tension between them.

The men took several helpings of the good food. Caroline noticed that the Ingalls boys had nice table manners. They kept their elbows off the table and didn't use their knives to pick their teeth, as Mr. Graylick did, and they complimented the ladies on their cooking.

"Caroline mentioned that you have a baby at home," Mother said to Peter when he came up to thank her for the food. "Is the child sickly?"

Peter shook his head. "Just a touch of colic," he replied. "But George is such a strong little man, and the girls dote on him so, I'm sure he'll be hale in no time."

Caroline wanted to ask how many sisters the Ingalls boys had, and if any were her age, but there wasn't time. Already Pa was clearing his throat and pushing back from the table.

"Better make hay while the sun shines," he said. The men clapped their hands together, thanked the ladies for a fine meal, and headed back to the fields.

Now the women sat and ate. Caroline thought the blackberry pie the Ingalls boys had brought tasted almost as good as Mother's pie. When they were finished eating, they took the platters of leftover food back into the kitchen out of the hot sun. They washed the dishes and set them to dry so they would be ready for supper. Then Mrs. Wigham and Mrs. Spivey brought out their sewing and knitting and sat with Mother in the parlor. Martha and Nell took Baby Daniel into the yard and played with him in the shade of a tall oak tree.

"C'mon Caroline, let's go to the field," Eliza pleaded. "I don't want to sit around like Martha and Nell do. All they ever talk about is when they will be married and how many babies they will have. I don't think I ever want to be married. I want to travel across the country like our Miss May."

Caroline looked back and forth from Eliza to Martha. Part of her wanted to stay with the older girls, and part of her wanted to go with Eliza. But then Mother settled the matter. She told Caroline to see that Thomas and Jamie were staying out of trouble. So Caroline followed Eliza past the barn and the garden and the field of corn. The afternoon sun was burning brightly overhead. Caroline pulled her calico bonnet farther over her face.

When they came to the edge of the field, Thomas and Jamie were there with their buckets of water ready for when the men called to them. Their cheeks bulged as they chewed on the wheat kernels they had stripped from the stalk.

"You two look like a couple of cows chewing their cud," Eliza said.

"Moo," said Jamie. Eliza giggled.

Thomas held out his hand. "Care for some?" he asked.

Eliza took a small pinch of the kernels and put them on her tongue, but Caroline shook her head. She knew it was not polite to talk and chew at the same time, and she had questions to ask Jamie, starting with, "How many sisters do you have?"

Jamie had to rearrange the large wad of wheat gum in his mouth before answering. "Too many. They're always trying to boss me."

"What are their names?"

"There's Lydia and Polly and Docia," Jamie answered, numbering them on his fingers.

Caroline repeated the pretty names to herself. "Are they all older than you?"

"Lydia is thirteen and Polly is eleven," Jamie said. "But Docia's only six."

"I guess you'll all be going to school then?" Caroline asked excitedly. She was happy to hear there would be two new girls near her own age.

Jamie gave a scowl. "I reckon Ma will make us go—all except for Hiram and George, 'cause they're too young. And Peter and Charlie because they're the oldest. They won't have to go till winter."

Thomas nodded his head and let out a loud sigh. "It's the same with us. I can't wait till I'm old enough to only go to school in the winter."

"I can't wait till I'm old enough not to go at all!" Jamie exclaimed.

"You're lucky to have a schoolhouse so close by," Caroline said. Right away she knew she sounded old and stuffy—like Mrs. Spivey. But she couldn't help it. She had known many years when there had been no school to attend. She had been happy when Mr. Kellogg had organized the town and built the schoolhouse. It was large enough for everyone, and even though she had not liked Mr. Crenshaw, she had been thankful to go every day.

"Aw, you sound like my ma," Jamie said. Then he turned and pointed across the field.

"Hey, look at them go!"

Caroline looked up to see Peter and Charlie, Joseph and Henry, and then Jacob come flying down their rows of wheat. Their cradles moved in a fast rhythm as they raced one another across the field. Their shirts were dark with sweat, and their hair was plastered against their necks under their straw hats.

It was thrilling to see the boys moving so quickly together, rocking their cradles back and forth and sending the golden wheat churning into the air. Caroline was glad she had come with Eliza and not stayed behind with Martha and Nell.

As Joseph pulled ahead of the others, Caroline found herself calling out for him to win, just as Thomas and Eliza were doing. She couldn't help jumping up and down when he finished his row first. After dropping his cradle to the ground and stretching out his arms and back, he turned toward Caroline and the others and waved his hat in the air. Peter and Charlie and Henry and Jacob finished their rows together, and quickly Jamie and Thomas shot forward to bring them water.

Slowly Caroline and Eliza walked back to the house. The ladies were still in the parlor. Baby Daniel was sleeping in a basket in the kitchen, and Martha had taken Nell upstairs to show her what the *Watertown Chronicle* was saying about bloomers. One article, dated only a few months before—May 15, 1851— read:

BOUND TO GO. —The new style of ladies' dresses is bound to go. It has been introduced into most of the eastern cities, and is fast working its way west. Some of the ladies of Kenosha, in this state, have already adopted it. These short dresses and pantaloons give the wearer, it is said, a sprightly appearance.

Another piece read,

THE NEW FASHION. —We saw a lady in Milwaukee, the other day, rigged in the new style. We are decidedly in favor

of it. It is a great improvement upon the old mop-the-street style of dresses, and not only ought to prevail, but will. There's no mistake about this. The ladies throughout the country are determined in the matter; and when the sex wills, "that's the end on't!"

"Mother could make us bloomers if she wanted," Eliza said. "She can make anything."

"Do you think she would?" Nell asked, breathless.

Martha shook her head, and Caroline had to agree. Mother liked to keep up as much as she could with the new styles, but she was also very practical. Even though the little farm was doing well now, there was no money for extras. The dresses Mother made for the girls were meant to last through many wearers—first Martha, then Caroline, then Eliza. She would not waste precious fabric on fleeting fads. Occasionally this made Caroline sad. Secretly she sometimes wished she was rich and lived in a city where a dressmaker made her the most fashionable dresses. But at the same time, it was hard to imagine living any other life but the one she knew.

Slowly the afternoon faded and the full moon began to rise through the trees. While the ladies went about the supper preparations, Caroline and Martha and Eliza saw to the evening chores. They fetched Baby and Bess from the woods and did the milking. They shooed the pig into his pen. They fed the chickens and geese and brought the firewood in from the woodpile.

Pa had told them that they would not stop for supper until all the wheat was stacked. So the ladies and girls ate by themselves and then kept the food warm until the men were through.

At last another great shout came up from the field. The wheat was cut. Now the workers went back over the field. They gathered the piles they had made with the cradles and worked them into tight bundles. Thomas and Jamie went running through the maze of shocked wheat, crisscrossing the field. They called out to the girls to chase them. Eliza rushed out right away. Caroline held back for a moment, but the newly cut field was so pretty in the moonlight, she picked up her skirts and dashed after her sister. Soon she heard giggles behind her, and she turned to see Nell and Martha following her. Charlie and Henry and Jacob were standing at the edge of the field, where they had dropped their cradles. They were grinning to see the girls running, but they were too tired from the day's work to join in. After a while they followed the men to the table to eat. Then Caroline and her sisters and Nell came to help serve up the late supper.

"A good day's work," Pa said. "I'm much obliged to you all."

"Hope the weather holds," Mr. Wigham said. Caroline knew he must be thinking about the wheat sitting in his own field. Tomorrow the men and boys would be cutting at his farm.

"I think it will," Pa said, eyeing the sky.

The moon was large and round, and the stars were twinkling brightly. They did not need candles or lanterns because everything was lit up almost as if it were day. After they finished eating, Pa and the other men sat back in their chairs, smoking their pipes while the ladies cleared the table. Everyone was quiet, enjoying the lovely night, until Charlie spoke up.

"Excuse me, sir," he said to Pa. "I brought my fiddle along. Mind if I play a tune or two?"

Pa looked surprised. "You play the fiddle, young man?" he asked, and Charlie answered "A little, sir."

Caroline exchanged glances with Martha and Eliza as Pa gave a quick nod of his head. "A little music would be most welcome long about now."

Charlie brought his fiddle box from where he had left it in the barn. They all waited while he tightened the strings and rosined up the bow. When he began to play, the notes came out slow and mournful. Caroline recognized the tune. It was "Cold Blows the Wind," one of Mother's favorites, and Mother's voice was the first to join in with the fiddle's voice to sing:

"Cold blows the wind to my true love,
And gently drops the rain.
I've never had but one true love,
And in greenwood he lies slain."

Other voices mingled with Mother's until the song came to its sad end.

"That sure was some pretty playing, son," Mr. Graylick said at last. "But I'm wondering if you can pluck a livelier tune."

Charlie grinned and let the fiddle give his answer. Quickly the notes came as the bow flew over the strings. Everyone began to clap and sing,

"Oh Susanna, don't you cry for me!
I'm going to California, with my washpan
on my knee!"

It was a song Caroline had heard many times over the past two years. Charlie said he had learned it from a fiddler who was headed west with other forty-niners in search of gold.

"Charlie can pick up any tune after he's heard it once," Peter said.

Charlie grinned at the compliment and continued to play song after lively song. Some were new tunes and some were old favorites. Caroline and the others clapped and sang to "Pop! Goes the Weasel" and "Old Dan Tucker" and "Weevily Wheat" and "Billy Boy." The music swirled around the clearing, but the night was growing very late. The moon was round and high in the velvet sky when the fiddle slowed and they sang the last song:

"In the starlight, in the starlight,
At the daylight's dewy close,
When the nightingale is singing
His last love song to the rose,
In the calm, clear light of summer
When the breezes softly play,
From the glitter of our dwelling
We will gently steal away."

The song came to an end and no one said a word for a time. Caroline noticed Nell and

Jacob gazing at each other. Eliza noticed it too. She elbowed Caroline and put her hand over her mouth to stifle her giggles. Caroline shook her head at her sister. She could see how silly Nell and Jacob looked, but she could also see why Nell was so smitten. Jacob was tall and handsome, with a quick smile and an easygoing manner.

At last Pa tapped his pipe on his heel and stretched his legs. "I'm mighty glad you brought your fiddle along, son," he said, and they all murmured the same.

Charlie's smile was bashful. "I'm mighty glad to have the chance to play for folks," he replied. "More often than not I end up playing for the birds." He found Caroline among the listeners and gave her a wink.

Caroline looked down at her hands resting in her lap. It felt strange to be the keeper of a secret for someone she hardly knew.

When she looked up again, the cradles were being put away and the ladies were collecting their pots and pans and baskets. Then the wagons were rolling off down the wagon path.

"See you tomorrow!" everyone called.

As the Ingalls boys got ready to go, Pa insisted on taking his rifle and walking them home.

"These woods are tamer than they used to be, but I still wouldn't want to be out after dark without my gun," Pa said.

The bright clearing seemed empty after the lively music. Caroline watched as Pa and the Ingalls boys disappeared into the shadowy woods; then she turned and followed her sisters inside. It had been a good day. And she was happy to have heard the fiddle again.

Our Miss May

The next day they all went by wagon to the Wighams' to help cut their wheat, and after that they went to the Spiveys'. Mr. Graylick had only a small crop of wheat, and the Ingallses would not have any until next year. Over the next few weeks Pa and the boys would go to their farms to help clear trees and make split-rail fences.

"I wish *we'd* been able to trade work when we were cutting down all those trees," Henry said wistfully one day.

"At least we have folks around now to help

with the harvest," Joseph said. He always looked on the bright side of every situation.

When Saturday came, Caroline was happy to stay home and do the baking. On Sunday she was glad to go to church and then to rest. The following week they were busy again, helping Mother with the cleaning. Mother was determined that the already spotless house should be sparkling for "our Miss May."

Monday they washed the curtains and the kitchen linen and beat the dust out of the rag rugs. Tuesday they blackened the stove and made sure all the dishes and the pots and pans were gleaming. Then they aired out the quilts and took the bedding apart and refilled the ticks with the good clean hay Pa and the boys had cut in August. They cleaned the glass windowpanes with vinegar and water, and they scrubbed the wide plank floors with sand from the river.

They made sure the little room where Miss May would sleep was cheerful with a lovely quilt and a piece of calico over the chest of drawers. The room was next to the kitchen, so it would be especially warm in the winter months.

At last, when Saturday arrived, the house was bright and shining, and so were Caroline and her brothers and sisters. They had had their Saturday-night baths on Friday night in order to be ready for Miss May. All that was left to do was the baking, and Mother had begun that at sunrise. Caroline and Eliza helped roll out the dough for pies and cookies, while Martha was in charge of the bread.

By noon they were ready for their guest. The house looked so lovely and smelled so good from all the baking, Caroline felt a sense of deep pride. She did not see how anyone could turn her nose up at such a happy home.

"Mr. Kellogg told us to expect them soon after dinner," Mother said when Eliza asked for the hundredth time when Miss May would arrive. Mr. Kellogg was the head of the school board. Miss May had sent him a letter saying that she would be arriving on Friday's coach. She would spend the evening at the inn Mr.

Kellogg had built in town with the money he had made in the California gold mines. Then he would bring her by wagon to Caroline's house.

"I wonder that she doesn't want to stay put in Mr. Kellogg's inn for the whole term," Henry said. "Fine digs, I'd say."

"The inn is for travelers on the stagecoach," Mother said. "It's no place for a lady to spend the entire school term."

After a quick dinner of bean soup and corn cakes, the girls went back upstairs to change out of their everyday dresses. They would not wear their best clothes, for those were only worn on Sunday and other very special occasions. They would put on their second best—the dresses they would wear to school. Caroline's was made out of deep-blue wool. It had been Martha's the year before. Mother had reworked the scalloped collar and added a band of dark red to the bottom. Martha's dress had been Mother's. It was a rich burgundy-colored wool with black trim along the bodice. Eliza's was red-and-black plaid and had been worn by both Martha and Caroline. Caroline always felt bad for Eliza, because her dresses had been worn by two sisters.

Caroline had just finished tying up her laces when she heard the sound of a wagon jingling down the wagon path.

"She's here! She's here!" Eliza exclaimed, dashing through the bedroom door and down the stairs. Mother caught her before she ran out into the yard.

"That is not the way to greet our guests," Mother scolded. She straightened Eliza's collar and turned to inspect the rest of the children, who had trooped downstairs. The boys had changed out of their work shirts and into their good blue-linen shirts. "I expect you all to be on your best behavior," Mother said, reaching out to smooth down Henry's unruly curls.

"Yes, ma'am," they all murmured.

"Good day to you, my friend!" They heard Mr. Kellogg's pleasant voice calling out, and Pa's easy reply, "And a good day to you, sir."

Mother led the way out the door as Mr. Kellogg was helping the teacher from her seat in the wagon.

"No bloomers," Eliza whispered loudly. Mother gave her a stern look.

Caroline saw the new arrival cock her head and give a quizzical half smile, but she said nothing until Mr. Kellogg had made the proper introductions. Then she took Mother's hand in her own and smiled warmly.

"How do you do?" she said in a clear, educated voice. "It is a pleasure to make your acquaintance."

Caroline saw at once that the new teacher was not pretty, exactly. Her features were too strong to be called pretty. She was a striking woman, with high cheekbones, a long nose, and large wide-set eyes that were looking wonderingly around. She was very tall—taller than Mother—with a long, slender waist.

It was true she did not wear bloomers, but her light-gray dress was fashionably cut, with a V-shaped bodice and a full skirt with a fringe

of black velvet. Around her shoulders she wore a short mantle with matching black-velvet fringe along the edges. Her sleeves were short and very wide, with white undersleeves of dainty lace. She wore black kid gloves and a high scalloped double collar of creamy lace. Her bonnet was small and stylish and sat toward the back of her head, its wide black-velvet ribbons tied in a large bow under her pointed chin. Her hair was black like Mother's and parted in the middle, softly framing her face.

Caroline thought she looked rather imposing as she stood straight and tall beside Mother, but as she came closer to say hello to each of the children in turn, Caroline saw that her smile was warm and her gray eyes were kind. And she was not as old as she initially appeared. Caroline guessed her to be in her early twenties.

"What fine-looking children," Miss May said.

"I think you'll find that they are all good scholars," Mr. Kellogg announced, giving

Caroline a special smile as he said the words. Mr. Kellogg knew Caroline particularly liked learning.

"It will be a pleasure to teach them, I'm sure. And it will be a pleasure to come to know one another." She turned back to Mother and Pa. "I hope it was not any trouble to board me."

"No trouble at all," Pa said, and Mother replied, "We are only too glad to have you."

Miss May had two large trunks and a satchel of dark-brown leather. The boys had carried them into the house as Mr. Kellogg announced that he must be going.

"I have no doubt that I am leaving you in the best of hands," Mr. Kellogg said. With that he climbed back into his wagon and drove away.

Mother showed Miss May to her room. Caroline followed. All at once she was nervous again that the new teacher, with her fine clothes, would not like their house.

But as she removed her bonnet and mantle and gloves, Miss May admired the quilt

Mother had made when she was a girl and the solid bedstead and handsome chest of drawers Pa had built.

Then she was ushered into the parlor.

"What a lovely room," she said.

Caroline glanced around and felt her confidence return. It *was* a lovely room, with the afternoon light streaming through the curtained glass windows. There was the daybed they had brought with them from Brookfield, and the two chairs Pa had made to match. Pa had also made a table and chairs set for one corner of the room and a chest to go between the windows. On the chest sat the mahogany clock Mother cherished because it had been Father's. On the floor was the rag rug Martha had made last year, and on the walls hung the samplers all the girls had made and framed themselves. The black iron stove sat in one corner of the room to keep them warm in the winter. It wasn't as fancy as Mr. Kellogg's house, but it was like home. Caroline could feel herself smiling, and she ducked her head so no one would see.

Mother served tea and fresh milk, and she cut large slices of her special blueberry cake and put them on the pewter dishes she kept for company.

"This cake is delightful, Mrs. Holbrook," Miss May said after taking a few dainty bites.

"Please call me Charlotte," Mother said.

"Then you must call me Patience," Miss May replied.

"What a perfect name for a teacher!" Mother exclaimed, and Miss May smiled.

"Yes, I have no doubt my father christened me with teaching in mind," she said. "We come from a long line of teachers. My father was a teacher, and his father before him was a schoolmaster in England. My brother and I have followed the same path."

"Then your brother teaches school as well," Pa said.

"He does—or rather, he did." Miss May paused and shook her head. "I am afraid the craze over the gold in California proved too much of a draw. Two years ago he gave up his books for the pick and the pan."

"Has he struck it rich?" Henry asked excitedly. Two years before, Henry had not been able to stop talking about gold. He had wanted to go out west when Mr. Kellogg had sent some men to pan for him, but Mother had insisted he was too young. Now he did not speak of it as much, but Caroline knew he still dreamed of going to California, or Oregon, where there were new gold mines.

"I am afraid William has not found gold." Miss May sighed. "Many have been captivated by the notion of a quick profit."

"Mr. Kellogg did all right," Henry mumbled, and Mother gave him a scolding look.

"Mr. Kellogg was a lucky man," Pa said mildly.

"In any case"—Miss May smiled—"I keep hoping William will come to his senses soon. He was a fine teacher."

As they continued to drink their tea and eat their cake, Miss May told them something of her journey. It had taken seven days to travel by packet through the Erie Canal from Albany to Buffalo. The packet boats were long and flat and were pulled along the shallow canal by mules. The mules walked on the shore, attached to the boats by long ropes.

"The mule drivers sing, and the pace is leisurely to say the least," Miss May explained. "But the boats glide along the water as if it were glass. And I met all manner of travelers. There were families from Norway and Finland and Germany who were new to this country. And there were those who were simply tired of living in the east and thought they would try their luck on the frontier. We all took turns sitting on the roof of the boat because it wasn't big enough for everyone at once. That way we could enjoy the fresh air and the beautiful New York landscape as it floated by. Quite a comfortable way to travel, all in all."

Caroline wondered what it would be like to sit in a small boat among so many people, all from different countries. She wasn't sure she would feel as comfortable as Miss May had felt.

After staying with friends in Buffalo overnight, Miss May had taken a steamer through the Great Lakes. It had taken another nine days to reach Milwaukee, where she had stayed overnight before taking the morning coach to Concord.

"Did you pass through Brookfield?" Martha asked.

"I believe we did have a brief stop there," Miss May replied.

"That's where we used to live," Caroline explained.

"Oh, I see," Miss May said. "It seemed to be a prosperous town."

"I've watched the stagecoach drive by," Thomas blurted out. "It goes fast!"

Miss May turned to him and smiled and nodded. "The stage does indeed go fast, young man," she said. "But the ride is quite bumpy and dusty, and the drivers pack as many bodies into one stage as they can. Not a very comfortable ride, I must say."

As Miss May continued to talk of the sights she had seen, Caroline suddenly remembered Mrs. Spivey's words. Miss May must indeed be a modern young woman, since she had traveled alone across miles and miles of unknown territory. It was hard to believe she had left her home to travel so far by herself.

Mother must have thought so too, for she asked, "Won't your mother and father worry that you have come here on your own?"

"My mother passed on when I was a baby," Miss May replied. "And my dear papa joined her this winter past."

"I am very sorry for your loss," Mother murmured. For a moment Miss May's gray eyes had a faraway look, and Caroline felt a rush of sadness. Caroline knew what it was like to lose a father.

"Well," Miss May continued in a cheerful voice, "my brother set off to see something of this great country of ours, and I have decided to do the same. I was happy when I saw Mr. Kellogg's advertisement in our newspaper, for my goal is to go where teachers are needed."

After all the tea and cake were gone, Pa and the boys went to bring the wheat in from the fields. They would store the shocks in the barn until they had time to do the threshing.

Mother said that the girls might show Miss May around the rest of the house.

As they went from room to room, the teacher was full of questions about their daily lives—what chores the girls were expected to do each day, and if they had favorite chores; what items around the house they had helped to make. She exclaimed over the rag rugs and the baskets Martha had woven and the quilts the girls had worked on together and the samplers they had made over the years. She was particularly interested in how Mother had decided to leave Brookfield and go farther west to buy her own land.

"Your mother is a brave woman," Miss May declared. "Did you know that in many states a woman still cannot purchase property in her own name?"

Caroline had not known this. Here she had been thinking of Miss May as modern, when Mother was already modern in her own right.

After they were finished touring the house, the girls led Miss May around the farm. They stopped first at the barn, which was built of smooth sanded planks just like the house but had a dirt floor. There were two stalls, one for the oxen and one for the cows, and there was a pen for the pig. A ladder led to the hayloft, where Henry was waiting for Joseph to hand him the next shock of wheat. The wheat would be stored aboveground along with the hay.

Pa tipped his straw hat and the boys nodded when Miss May stepped inside the barn, but they did not stop to chat. Pa had said there was rain in the air, and he wanted to get all the shocks in while the day was still clear. Pa knew it was going to rain because his bad leg ached.

The girls led Miss May to the first stall, where Slow and Ready were standing. The oxen lifted their large heads and blew through their flaring nostrils.

"They think we have something for them to eat," Eliza explained. She went to the corner of the barn, where they kept the grain, and poured some into Miss May's outstretched hand. The oxen pressed against the walls of their stall, straining their necks to reach for the treat. Miss May let out a laugh as their large tongues lolled along her palm.

"I am a city girl, you see," Miss May said. "I have much to learn from living here with you and your family."

Now it felt important to show Miss May around the little farm. Caroline had never thought that there would be anything to teach a teacher.

After the barn they went to the garden and told Miss May what vegetables were in which rows, and what herbs they had planted. They took her to the wheat field and explained about the cutting. They showed her the little cabin they had first lived in, which was now Pa's woodworking shed.

At last they came to the honeybee farm. Martha explained they had begun to keep honeybees two years before. At first there had been only one skep, but now there were four. It was Thomas' job to keep an eye on the bees. Soon they would be breaking open the skeps to see how much honey the bees had made that year.

Caroline felt a little guilty about the honeybee farm. When they opened the skeps, some of the bees would no longer have a home, and so they would die when the cold weather came. But the honey was wonderful, and this year they might even make money selling some at the general store. So it was hard to feel guilty for long.

"Did you know that honeybees are not indigenous to North America?" Miss May asked as they watched a line of bees make its way from the nearby flowers to the skep.

"What does indigenous mean?" Eliza asked.

Caroline was about to answer, but she did not want to sound like a show-off, so she waited for Miss May's reply.

"Indigenous means living naturally in an area," Miss May said. "Honeybees were brought to this country by the English."

"You mean they brought all the bees from England with them?" Eliza asked, wide-eyed.

Miss May smiled and shook her head. "No, they brought a few honeybees with them when they came here, and the honeybee thrived and multiplied. This honeybee here"—she pointed to one that buzzed close by—"is a direct descendent of an English honeybee."

"Just like us," Eliza said. "We were born here, but we come from Scotland."

"That's where our Grandma and Grandpa Tucker are from," Caroline said, speaking of Mother's parents.

Miss May nodded her head. "Exactly."

When they got back to the house, Miss May took them into her room and said, "You've been kind enough to show me around your home. Now it's my turn to show you something of mine."

Caroline and Martha and Eliza sat expectantly on the edge of the bed as Miss May took two keys from a little chain she wore around her neck and unlocked one of the trunks. When she opened the lid, Caroline saw that the trunk was entirely full of books and periodicals.

Her mouth opened in surprise. She did not know one person could own so many books.

"You see, I am always at home when I have my books around me," Miss May said.

Caroline was breathless looking at those books, but when she glanced at Martha and Eliza, she could tell they were a little disappointed.

"Do you like to read?" Miss May asked, her gray eyes focusing on Caroline.

"Oh, yes, we do," Caroline spoke up quickly. For some reason she did not want Miss May to think that her sisters would not appreciate the books. "Sometimes we read at night after supper. But we haven't had anything new in a long time."

"Perhaps we could choose something to read for this evening," Miss May suggested, bringing a few of the books out and laying them on the bedside table.

"Oh, yes," Caroline said again, but she wasn't sure how they would begin to choose. There were books she recognized from school, like the plays of William Shakespeare and

the poems of Whittier. But there were titles
she did not know. *Jane Eyre* by Currer Bell.
The House of the Seven Gables by Nathaniel
Hawthorne. A slim volume by Edgar Allan
Poe. *Moby-Dick* by Herman Melville.

"Have you heard of this man?" Miss May
asked, bringing out a small book with a plain
cover and simple writing along the front, which
read, *Narrative of the life of Frederick Douglass,
An American Slave, Written by Himself.*

The girls shook their heads.

"I myself have heard this man speak on the
horrors of slavery," Miss May said. "He is a
powerful orator."

"Are you an abolitionist?" Caroline asked.
She knew she was showing off using such a big
word, but Miss May just nodded.

"You are aware of the abolitionist movement,
then?" she asked.

"Oh yes," Caroline said. "Uncle Elisha is
one. He believes that slavery is wrong and
should be abolished."

Martha told Miss May about Uncle Elisha

and Aunt Margaret and the cousins and Grandma, who all lived in Milwaukee. Uncle Elisha was a newspaperman. He often wrote about slavery, and he and Aunt Margaret frequently attended abolitionist meetings.

"How very interesting," Miss May said. "Have you ever visited your family in Milwaukee?"

"No, but someday we will. Mother said so," Eliza replied matter-of-factly.

Next Miss May took out some periodicals and spread them on the bed. Now Martha and Eliza were more interested. There were new issues of *Godey's*, but there were also publications that Caroline had never seen before. One was called *Harper's Monthly Magazine*, and another was titled *Knickerbocker*.

Miss May pulled out one that was called *The Lily*. "This journal was started by Amelia Bloomer," she said. "Have you heard of her?"

"Oh yes!" the girls exclaimed.

"We thought you might be wearing bloomers," Eliza said.

Miss May's eyes twinkled. "Is that what you were whispering to your sister when you first came out of the house?"

Eliza blushed pink. "I didn't mean to whisper," she said.

"Well, as a matter of fact, I used to wear bloomers in Albany, but I did not know how they were being received out here."

"Do you have a pair?" Eliza asked excitedly.

"I am afraid I left them behind in Albany," Miss May said, and the girls sighed in disappointment. "It is too bad bloomers have been met with such animosity," Miss May continued. "As I was traveling, I couldn't help but think how much more comfortable and practical it would be to wear trousers."

Caroline exchanged glances with her sisters. What would Mrs. Spivey have to say about Miss May's opinions if she could hear!

The girls spent the rest of the afternoon with Miss May. Caroline was thrilled to look through the many books, and Martha and Eliza were excited to hear stories of Albany and New York City. Miss May had been to see the great actor Edwin Booth perform at the National Theatre. And she had heard Jenny Lind sing.

"She does indeed deserve to be called the Swedish Nightingale," Miss May said.

She had also been to all kinds of exhibitions, where she had seen many new inventions. "It is a wondrous age in which we are living," she exclaimed, telling them of the new machine invented by Mr. Howe that could actually sew smaller stitches than a human hand could make.

"I bet Mother's stitches are smaller!" Eliza boasted, and they told her about how Mother had been a dressmaker in Boston.

"She would be interested in these clever things, then," Miss May said, reaching into the satchel and bringing out a small velvet pouch. She poured several small golden pins into the palm of her hand for the girls to see. "These are called 'safety pins' because of this clasp here," she explained, showing them how the point of the pin tucked neatly into a little sleeve.

"How remarkable!" Mother said after they had called her in to see. And Mother's eyes shone when they lit upon all the books and periodicals.

Caroline told her that Miss May had offered to read to them that very night. "What a treat!" Mother said.

When it was time to do the evening chores, Caroline could hardly pull herself away from Miss May, but she knew they must not tire her out. Caroline saw to the hens and geese, then helped Mother with supper. It was a special meal since they had company. There was roasted wild turkey with corn bread stuffing and mashed turnips and bread and cranberry relish and honey. After all that there was blackberry pie. Miss May told Mother she had not eaten so well since leaving Albany.

They quickly cleared the table and wiped the dishes and put them away. Caroline was eager to see what Miss May would read to them first.

In the parlor Mother had Miss May sit in the most comfortable chair and set the oil lamp close so that she would have enough light to read by. Miss May held up a small, thin book bound in rich, dark leather. Along the front, in gold lettering, was the single word *Poems*.

"This is a new collection by Henry Wadsworth Longfellow, who is quite a favorite back east," Miss May said.

"Ah, yes," Mother said, "we are familiar with his name." And Caroline suddenly remembered the name from some of the magazines Uncle Elisha sent their way from time to time.

Mother settled into her chair and took up her knitting, and Martha and Eliza did the same. Caroline pretended to focus on the tiny stitches she must make for the new apron she was sewing, but she was too excited. Pa sat near the window, smoking his pipe while the boys whittled kindling.

Miss May brought the book close to the light and began to read in a clear, expressive voice. The poem was called *Evangeline*, and instantly Caroline was plunged into a world that seemed somehow familiar and yet completely unknown:

"This is the forest primeval. The murmuring
pines and the hemlocks,
Bearded with moss, and in garments green,
indistinct in the twilight,
Stand like Druids of eld, with voices sad
and prophetic,
Stand like harpers hoar, with beards that
rest on their bosoms.
Loud from its rocky caverns, the deep-voiced
neighboring ocean
Speaks, and in accents disconsolate answers
the wail of the forest."

As Miss May continued to read, Caroline came to understand that the forest was not the Wisconsin woods she knew but a place that existed long ago and far away. The setting was Nova Scotia, and Evangeline was a beautiful young French Canadian farm girl who was engaged to be married to her childhood sweetheart, the handsome and brave Gabriel.

At first the poem appeared to be a love story, and Caroline saw Henry and Thomas roll their eyes. But soon English warships were attacking and the poor villagers were engaged in a bloody battle. Caroline noticed her brothers had stopped their whittling to listen, sitting forward slightly in their seats. The English destroyed Evangeline's village and drove the Acadians, as the settlers were called, out of their homeland. Evangeline searched everywhere for Gabriel but could not find him among the living or the dead.

Suddenly, at this sad juncture, Miss May stopped reading. The only sound was the solemn ticking of the mahogany clock. Both Martha and Eliza had stopped their work. Even Mother's knitting needles were still. Caroline glanced quickly at Miss May, wondering why she had paused.

Miss May cleared her throat. "That is the end of the first part," she said. "It is a long poem, and it has grown late. Perhaps you would like to wait and hear the rest another night?"

It seemed to take Mother a moment to find her voice. "Oh, yes," she said. "What a good idea. We shall look forward to the next instalment." She smiled. "Thank you for such fine reading. What a powerful tale!"

"Yes, indeed," Pa added.

They all thanked Miss May and said good night. Caroline followed her sisters upstairs in a daze. Her head was full of Evangeline's tale, and she did not see how she could sleep. She knew that they would have to wait two more days to hear more of the story. Tomorrow was Sunday, and only the Bible would be read.

As she put on her nightgown, she thought of how some of the words in the poem had been difficult to follow. But Miss May had read in such a passionately expressive voice, Caroline had been able to grasp the meaning even when she did not completely understand what was being said. But one thing she did understand very clearly: They were very lucky Miss May had come to stay with them for a time. And that she had brought so many books.

School Begins

No matter how much Caroline liked school, the first day always made her stomach feel fluttery. It was a little frightening to go into a room full of people, even if there were friends from previous terms attending. And Caroline always wanted to make a good first impression upon the teacher. Now that the teacher was boarding in her own house, Caroline especially wanted to be on her best behavior.

"We'd better hurry," Caroline said as soon as she awoke Monday morning. "We must not be late with Miss May here."

Eliza was quick to jump out of bed and put on her dress and brush and braid her hair, but Martha moved more slowly. Caroline noticed that she did not smile and her eyes looked tired, as if she had not slept well. Caroline guessed that, as usual, Martha did not want to start school. On the first day last term Martha had asked Mother if she could stay home to help her in the house. Caroline knew she would never make such a plea with Miss May there. But still Caroline could tell she was not happy to go to school.

After Caroline was dressed, she did her morning chores quickly. When she came back from feeding the hens and geese, Miss May was helping Martha to set the table. Martha seemed more relaxed, and Miss May gave Caroline such a warm, encouraging smile, she felt her first-day worries melt away.

When breakfast was over and the dishes had been wiped and put away, Caroline hurried to put on her shawl and bonnet and take the dinner pail she shared with Martha and Eliza.

"A fine morning," Miss May said as they stepped into the yard, and Caroline answered right away, "Oh, yes, ma'am," because suddenly it *was* a fine morning—a perfect autumn morning. The air was crisp, and the sky overhead was a brilliant blue. The first rays of sunshine were setting the newly changing leaves afire with color. All around the house there were brand-new patches of crimson and yellow and orange.

"Whoa," Pa called to the oxen as he brought the wagon to a halt in front of the house. He helped Miss May onto the wagon seat with her leather satchel and the dinner basket Mother had fixed for her. Caroline scooted into the back of the wagon with Martha, Eliza, and Thomas.

"This ain't so bad," Thomas said under his breath as Pa set the wheels to turning.

"This *isn't* so bad," Caroline corrected, glancing at Miss May's back. She did not want the teacher to think her brother was so rough and uneducated that he used "ain't."

"That's what I said. This isn't so bad,"

Thomas whispered, giving a grin that made Caroline smile in spite of wanting to appear stern.

It wasn't bad at all, riding to school with the teacher. It was the very first time Caroline had ever ridden to school in the wagon. They had always walked, and they would be walking again tomorrow. Miss May had insisted that Pa not go to the trouble of driving her to the schoolhouse every single day. But on this first morning they needed to carry a pot of coals from their own stove to start the fire in the schoolhouse stove. The coals sat in a bucket in between Martha and Caroline. Every now and then they would carefully peer in to make sure the coals were still glowing.

As they jingled out of the clearing and down the wagon path, the sun disappeared except for little specks and patches of sunlight here and there. It was always darker and colder inside the woods, with the trees towering overhead. Instantly Caroline's thoughts went to *Evangeline*.

"This is the forest primeval." She said the

words to herself, trying to recall the other opening lines. Something about murmuring pines, bearded with moss, standing like Druids of eld.

Here the pines were murmuring very softly, the morning breeze rustling through the branches. Some of the trunks were covered in moss as if they were wearing green beards. Caroline supposed many of these trees had been standing for a hundred years or more. Trees were ancient things, and Caroline could see why the poet would call them Druids. Druids were an ancient order of priests. Miss May had explained that when Eliza had asked.

Caroline wondered if Miss May was thinking about the poem too. She sat very tall on the wagon seat beside Pa, but she kept looking to her right and left and above at the canopy of leaves overhead. Caroline tried to imagine what it was like to see the woods for the very first time. She remembered that when she had first come here, the woods had seemed to swallow everything up. Now she liked the comfort of the trees around her, surrounding her like some kind of fortress.

When they arrived at the Territorial Road, there were no other wagons, but as they neared town, they passed the new cabins and wood-frame houses that had been built over the last year. Folks were going about their morning chores, and a few stopped to wave as the wagon rolled by. Caroline smiled and waved back. It felt important to be traveling with the smartly dressed teacher. Miss May wore the same stylish gray dress and mantle and bonnet she had worn when she had first arrived.

At the crossroads they turned right at Mr. Kellogg's inn. The inn was a handsome two-story building made of planks that had been painted a cheery white. It had blue curtains at the windows and a large friendly porch with benches and chairs. Caroline knew that men often gathered there to visit and play checkers or chess.

Across from the inn sat the new general store, with the words

JAYSON'S DRY GOODS

painted across the large glass windows. Mr.
Jayson was out front, sweeping the porch. He
waved and called out, "Good morning," as
they passed. After the general store there was
a blacksmith's shop and the little church Pa
had helped to build.

And that was the town of Concord. It was
not very big, but with two shops, an inn, and a
church, it was much bigger than it had been
when Caroline had first arrived. The mill Pa
had helped to raise was not in the town itself
but a little ways off, through the woods.

When the wagon came around a small bend
in the road, they could see Mr. Kellogg's grand
home high atop Concord Hill. Its many windows sparkled in the morning sun.

"I can't wait to see Margaret," Eliza whispered. Margaret Kellogg was nearly Eliza's
age, and they had become special friends.

Pa turned the wagon off the Territorial
Road, and they went through a small patch of
woods. The schoolhouse was in the middle
of a large clearing—the same clearing where
Caroline had attended a Camp Meeting almost

two years before. Like most of the clearings in these parts, the land was dotted with tree stumps, and the children often played jump the stump or king of the stump at recess. The schoolhouse itself was a tall, narrow, one-room building made of unpainted pine planks. It had a pointed roof, and from the front it did not appear to have any windows at all, only a large double door made out of solid oak. But Caroline knew that there were tall glass windows running along both sides of the building. She always liked to sit near one of those windows.

Pa pulled up right in front of the door and stopped the wagon. He helped Miss May down with her basket and satchel. Then he carefully lifted out the pot of coals and set them on the front steps of the school.

"I reckon I'll be off, then," he said with a quick nod.

Miss May thanked him for the ride, and Caroline and the others called good-bye. Pa would not stay to help light the stove inside the schoolhouse. That was Miss May's job, since she was the teacher. And it was the children's job to help bring in the wood from the shed around back and do any other little thing that needed doing. Boarding the teacher did not just mean keeping her but helping her with chores before and after school as well.

For a moment Miss May stood looking up at the schoolhouse. Then she took a key out of her skirt pocket, unlocked the front door, and stepped inside. The small entryway where they would keep their coats and shawls and dinner pails was dark, but as soon as they passed through it, they saw the sunlight streaming through the windows, making the pine walls and floor glow a golden yellow.

The desks sat in neat rows all the way from the back to the front, where the teacher's desk perched on a raised platform just below the blackboard. There were aisles along the sides of the desks and a wider one down the middle. The stove and woodbox sat in the very center of the room, and the seats closest to it were always the most popular in winter.

Miss May set them all to work right away.

Martha and Caroline swept down the aisles and inside the entryway while Thomas and Eliza brought in the wood to fill the woodbox. During the fall and winter terms, families were supposed to bring a stack of firewood for each child they sent to school. Pa and the boys had hauled four stacks to the woodshed the week before. When Henry and Joseph came to school the next term, they would haul six.

After the room was tidy and the stove had been lit, Miss May said, "Since you are the first to arrive, you may choose your seats."

Thomas chose a seat on the boys' side near the front since he was younger, but not too far from the stove. Caroline and Martha chose a place on the girls' side near the windows and toward the back, since they were older, and Eliza sat in the middle.

Quietly they put their school things on the little shelf that had been built right under the desk. Thomas and Eliza had slates and pieces of chalk, and they each had a reader that had been Mother's long ago. Caroline and Martha shared the brand-new *McGuffey's Eclectic Reader* that Uncle Elisha had sent from Milwaukee last year. It had a cheery yellow cover with a handsome pattern of vines and flowers across the front. Besides their reader they had slates and chalk like Thomas and Eliza, but since they were older, they also had the notebooks and pens and ink they had made themselves.

The notebooks were made from the rough brown paper Mother always saved after they had bought something at the general store. Caroline and Martha had taken several sheets of paper and folded them over. They had sewn the sheets together with thread and then carefully drawn straight lines across the pages. They had sewn covers for the notebooks out of pieces of plain cotton from Mother's rag bag.

The pens were really goose quills they had plucked from the cranky geese a few weeks before. The ink had been made from maple trees. Long ago, Mother had shown them how to take the bark and boil it in a kettle with a little water to make a black liquid. Then they added a powder called copperas that Pa brought from the general store. It made the liquid thicker. They kept the ink in a little ink bottle that had been Mother's when she was a girl.

After they had put their things away, they sat with their hands on their desks. Thomas began to fidget, and Eliza kept glancing back at Caroline and Martha. It was strange to be sitting in the nearly empty schoolhouse so early in the morning. Caroline almost felt like giggling from nervousness, and she could tell that Martha did too.

Miss May looked through the large black ledger that Mr. Crenshaw had left, with all the scholars' names written in it and notes about their progress the year before. Then she arranged the schoolbooks she had brought: her own copies of various McGuffey's readers and primers and spellers, a dictionary, and a Bible. After that she brought out a small book with a marbled cover and a pen and a bottle of ink. She began to write in the little book, and Caroline couldn't help wondering what she was writing.

At last Caroline heard a muffled yell from across the school yard, and then another and another. It sounded as if the schoolhouse were being attacked by a very small, very loud army. Thomas turned in his seat, and a look of pure agony passed over his face. Caroline knew he wanted to rush out to meet his friends. Miss May knew it as well. She looked up from her writing, and her gray eyes were laughing.

"You are free to do as you like until I ring the bell," she said.

Thomas just managed a "thank you, ma'am" before he lunged out of his seat and rushed down the aisle and out the door. Eliza followed more slowly, but Martha wanted to wait for her friends inside, and Caroline decided to stay with her. Caroline kept glancing at Miss May as she continued to write in her little book. Caroline noticed that the pen she was using had a pearl handle that was shaped like a feather.

In a little while, the friends Caroline and Martha had made over the last few terms began to arrive. There were the sisters Hilda and

Birgitta Nielsen, who had come to America when they were babies and spoke with only a slight German accent. They took the desk in front of Caroline and Martha. Alice Potts, whose father worked for Mr. Kellogg, and Maddy Jayson, the storekeeper's daughter, shared the desk in front of them. There were Mary Pratt and Libby Atwood. The Atwoods would be boarding Miss May next term, and Caroline could tell Libby was excited to get a look at the teacher. Nell Spivey arrived in a rush and took the seat right next to Martha, and they began whispering. Caroline was sure Martha was telling all about the bloomers. She saw Nell's eyes sweep over Miss May approvingly.

"Here, Docia," a voice said, making Caroline turn in her seat. "You know you'll have to sit up front with the little girls. It's no use pouting."

Although she had never laid eyes on them before, Caroline knew instantly that the three girls standing nearby were the Ingalls sisters. Docia appeared to be about six years old, and she had a very stubborn expression on her pretty face. She wore a smart little dress of blue-and-cream-colored gingham. She looked very much like her brother Charlie. Her eyes were a deep blue, and her thick hair was dark and curly under her bonnet. The older girls looked more like Jamie, with soft brown hair and brown eyes. They wore neat calico dresses and matching bonnets. Caroline wondered if they were as nice as their brothers.

The oldest sister took Docia to a desk near the front. When she returned, she was shaking her head. "Really, Docia is so impossible these days." Then they looked around for a seat.

"This one is free," Caroline spoke up, pointing to the desk directly behind her.

"Thank you," the younger girl said politely. "I'm Polly Ingalls, and this is my sister Lydia."

"I know," Caroline said, then quickly explained. "I mean, I couldn't help but hear you call your sister Docia. I'd heard your names already, you see. Your brothers came to help us with our wheat. I'm Caroline Quiner."

Polly's face lit up. "Oh yes, Charlie told us all about you. We didn't know we had neighbors so close by."

Caroline introduced Polly and Lydia to the other girls, but there wasn't time to get acquainted. Miss May was walking down the aisle, carrying the school bell in one hand. She smiled and said, "Good morning, young ladies," as she passed by on her way outside. Caroline heard the clanging of the bell, then the loud clomping of boots and the shout of voices as the boys and girls came streaming through the door in a rush of noise. As soon as Miss May came back inside, the room fell silent. Caroline saw that Eliza was sitting next to Margaret, and Thomas had found Jamie Ingalls.

"Good morning, scholars," Miss May said in her clear voice. She turned and wrote her name on the blackboard; then her large gray eyes swept over the room. Her manner was businesslike but friendly. "I am your new teacher. My name is Miss May. I am looking forward to getting to know each and every one of you over the next few months."

Caroline glanced around the room. No one, not even the bigger boys, was fidgeting or making faces as they sometimes did with a new teacher. Caroline hoped it would stay that way.

Now that school had begun, the morning went by quickly. One by one they all went to the front to tell Miss May their names and how far along they were in their studies. When it was Caroline's turn, Miss May seemed very pleased with Caroline's progress in the new McGuffey.

"Mr. Kellogg was right. You seem to be a fine scholar," Miss May said.

"Thank you," Caroline replied, blushing a little.

After Miss May had written all the names in the ledger, she set the older scholars to copying from their readers while she went among the small girls and boys to help them with their ABC's.

Caroline and Martha sharpened their quills with the little knife Pa had given them and dipped the points into the ink. They began to copy the selection Miss May had chosen. It was Patrick Henry's famous speech, and Caroline felt a shiver of awe as she wrote the final words: "Give me liberty or give me death." The words made her think of the brave men who had fought the British to make America its own country.

When Miss May had finished with the younger boys and girls, she walked among the desks, commenting on the older scholars' work. She complimented Caroline on her penmanship and gently gave Martha a few suggestions on how to make her lines a little straighter.

Then there was recess, and after recess there was reading. The younger scholars who knew their letters took turns reading aloud a story about a lame dog. Then the older scholars read from what they had copied.

Last year Caroline had hated reading. Whenever any scholar had said a word incorrectly, Mr. Crenshaw had made fun. He would screw up his face and mimic the way the scholar had mispronounced the word. Miss May did not make fun. She simply corrected the girl or boy and then had the whole class pronounce the word, as if they all needed to learn the lesson.

It made the person who had made the mistake not feel so bad.

After reading, it was time for noon recess. Caroline and Martha took their dinner pails and shawls and bonnets from the shelves in the entryway and went outside. Even though it was chilly, the sunshine made it feel warm. The older girls found a grassy spot and sat down to eat. Caroline had forgotten all about her nervousness from the morning. It was nice to sit and talk with the other girls. Caroline especially liked Polly. She had a wonderful smile that made her whole face light up. And she was interested in hearing more about Miss May. When Caroline told her about the trunk full of books, Polly looked excited.

"Do you think she will read to us in school?" Polly asked.

"Maybe she will," Caroline said.

"Oh, I hope so," Polly exclaimed, and Caroline realized she had found a friend who liked books as much as she did.

When recess was over, Miss May stood at the door and rang the bell. Then there were arithmetic and geography, grammar and spelling. Next to reading and writing, spelling was Caroline's favorite lesson. She spelled all the words Miss May gave her correctly, even "ascendancy," which had "c"'s in it that were pretending to be "s" sounds.

When the last hour of the day drew near, Miss May had them close their books.

"We shall now play a game," she said.

A buzz went through the room. A game? Caroline had never played games during lessons, and neither had anyone else.

"Quiet now, scholars," Miss May admonished, but her lips were turned up in a smile. "I believe that learning is not all work. It can be fun, too. To demonstrate this, we shall play the game of clap or hiss."

Miss May divided the room into two teams, and she gave the teams leaders. Caroline was the leader of one team, and Maddy Jayson was the leader of the other since they were the only two in school who had spelled all their words correctly. Martha was on Maddy's team, but Eliza and Thomas were on Caroline's.

"Now, one team shall choose a verb in secret," Miss May explained. "And the other team will have to guess and perform what that verb is. If one team guesses correctly, the other team will clap. But if they are not correct, you must hiss. In order to communicate, you must only clap or hiss. You cannot speak. If you do, you will forfeit your team's turn."

After she was done explaining the rules, Miss May had Maddy's team go out into the entry-way. Then she told Caroline to choose a verb.

"What verb shall I choose?" Caroline asked. Her voice sounded small to her own ears. She was not sure she liked being the leader, because everyone was staring at her expectantly.

"Well," Miss May said gently, "that is for you and your team to decide."

Caroline felt a little dizzy, but then she caught sight of Polly smiling at her. "Walk," Caroline said. It was the first verb that popped into her head.

"Good," Miss May said. "Now we must think of a word that rhymes with 'walk.'"

Polly raised her hand, and Miss May nodded to her. "Chalk," Polly said.

"Good," Miss May said again. She went to the door and called for Maddy. "The first team has decided on a verb. It rhymes with the word 'chalk.'"

Maddy went back into the entryway to discuss what the verb could be with her teammates. When she returned, Miss May asked if her team was ready.

"Yes, ma'am," Maddy replied. Then several of the boys from Maddy's team held their arms up as if they were carrying rifles and moved stealthily down the center aisle toward their imagined prey. They thought the verb was "stalk."

Tentatively Caroline hissed, and then the other team members joined in. The boys looked so silly, and it was so strange to be hissing, that Caroline wanted to giggle, but she knew it was not right to giggle during schooltime. But then Nell did giggle, and so did Margaret, and Miss May did not reprimand them. Soon everyone was giggling. But no one spoke, so they continued the game.

Maddy's team had to return to the entryway again to discuss what the verb could be. When they came out, they all began to chatter amongst themselves. They now thought the verb was "talk." Once more Caroline's team hissed. On their next try, Lydia and Martha and Maddy joined hands and strolled slowly down the aisle. They were walking, and so Caroline and the others loudly clapped their hands.

The teams switched places, and it was Caroline's turn to guess and mime. The word Maddy's team had chosen rhymed with "soil." Caroline was sure the word was "boil," but how exactly did one mime boiling something?

"We'll pretend Miss May's desk is the stove," Polly said when they were planning in the entryway, "and we'll use the basket she keeps erasers in as the pot. We can use a ruler as a spoon so it will look like we're stirring something."

"That's a good idea," Caroline said. She felt grateful to Polly for being so quick-witted.

"Now who's going to do the boiling?" Jamie wanted to know.

Caroline looked around. She realized the boys did not want to do it because boiling something on a stove was woman's work. And none of the girls wanted to do it because they were shy.

"I'll do it," Caroline said at last. She did not want to, but she knew she must since Miss May had made her the leader.

The others stood huddled in the back as Caroline walked down the center aisle to Miss May's desk. Caroline felt all eyes upon her, and she knew her cheeks were turning pink. It seemed to take forever to put the basket on the desk and take up Miss May's ruler and pretend to stir a boiling stew. The room was silent for several seconds. Before anyone had a chance to clap or hiss, suddenly little Freddy Potts shouted out, "She's boilin' somethin'!" His eyes went wide and he put a hand over his mouth. The whole room burst into laughter, and several boys booed and pushed at Freddy. Miss May quieted them down.

"I am afraid, Freddy, that your outburst means that your team must forfeit their turn to Caroline's team," Miss May said.

Caroline felt relieved that she wouldn't have to continue pushing the ruler around inside the basket. Maddy had to tell that their verb was "toil," and her team had to go back out into the entryway and wait until Caroline's team had chosen a new verb.

As the game continued, Caroline forgot about being nervous and feeling silly. The game was fun, and it was a new way to think about verbs.

The final hour flew by, and suddenly Miss May was bringing the class to order. Caroline's team had won because they had never talked out loud as Freddy had done. Miss May thanked them all for a fine first day and then dismissed school.

They had been having so much fun, Caroline could hardly believe school was over. Polly waved good-bye as she left with Lydia and Docia and Jamie.

"See you tomorrow!" Polly called.

Caroline wished she could walk home with

Polly, but at the same time she was proud to stay and help Miss May tidy up. She would not have to do it every day. Some days there would be scholars who had come in late or not done their lessons. Then they would help wash the blackboard and sweep the floors.

After everything had been put in order, Caroline and Martha and Eliza and Thomas all walked home with Miss May through the late-afternoon woods.

The birds were singing, and the rabbits and chipmunks dashed through the grass and bushes. The squirrels ran chattering up the trunks of trees. Miss May asked if they ever saw bears.

"Oh, yes," Thomas said. "Now's the time to keep a lookout, because the bears are stuffing themselves, getting ready to sleep the whole winter long."

Just then there was a rustling nearby. Miss May's gray eyes darted quickly toward the sound.

"That could be a bear now!" Thomas exclaimed, and Miss May stopped in her tracks.

In the next instant Wolf came bounding through the trees. He let out a cheerful bark and trotted up to Caroline, giving her hand a lick in greeting before darting back into the woods.

Martha reached out and took Thomas by the ear and twisted it so that he let out a "Yeow!"

"Thomas is just trying to scare you," Martha said to Miss May. "We don't see bears nearly so much anymore. Pa says they don't like how civilized the woods are now."

"Aw, it's not so civilized," Thomas grumbled, but he moved far away from Martha as he spoke. "Henry and I saw a bear down by the river just last week. And sometimes you see panthers and wolves, too."

"Oh, you don't see panthers and wolves in the middle of the day," Martha said crossly. Then she turned to Miss May and smiled a reassuring smile. "And Pa keeps a rifle over the door just in case."

Miss May nodded, but Caroline could tell she did not feel totally reassured.

"Anyway, aren't there bears in Albany?" Thomas asked.

"Oh, I think bears would find Albany much too civilized for their taste," Miss May said with a half smile.

As they continued to walk, Caroline noticed that Miss May glanced quickly at any rustling along the path, but she did not look too nervous. After a while she said, "This truly is beautiful country. I can see why so many wish to come here."

When they reached home, Mother said she did not have to ask them how school went.

"I can tell by your faces that you enjoyed your first day," she said.

"Oh, yes," Caroline breathed.

"It wasn't so bad," Thomas admitted.

"And that is high praise indeed, coming from our Thomas," Mother said, laughing.

"I will take it as such," Miss May said with a smile.

Harvest Days

Each day Caroline liked Miss May more and more. She was such a good teacher that even Martha did not seem to mind school that much. She worked harder at her lessons than she had ever done before.

In the afternoons Miss May continued to surprise the class with word games and puzzles. On Fridays they had spelldowns, and Caroline was always the last one standing. And just as Polly had hoped, Miss May sometimes read to them from her collection of books. The boys liked the selections Miss May chose from

Moby-Dick because the novel was about sailors on a great adventure in search of a monstrous white whale. Caroline and Polly liked *Jane Eyre*, especially when Miss May told the class that Currer Bell was a pseudonym and the writer was actually thought to be a woman.

"I think I would like to write a novel or a poem one day," Polly sighed as they ate their dinner together at recess one afternoon. "But I'm not so good a writer as you."

Caroline looked up in surprise. It was true that she enjoyed writing and that she had received high marks on the compositions Miss May had had them write and read to the class from time to time. But Caroline had never once thought about writing a novel or a poem.

"I wouldn't know what to write about," Caroline said.

"Oh, you could write about growing up here in Wisconsin," Polly said.

Caroline thought for a moment. "That doesn't seem interesting enough for a whole novel. It's not like growing up in an orphanage and then going off to work as a governess for a mysterious man in a great house."

"Well, maybe you could meet a mysterious man here," Polly said, giggling a little. "And you could fall madly in love and go west."

Polly was a few months younger than Caroline, but in some ways she seemed older.

"I don't think I want to go west," Caroline said simply. "I like it right here."

But Polly's words stayed with Caroline. Between school and home Caroline was hearing many stories. She wondered how writers thought up the tales they told.

At home it had taken a whole week of evening readings to get through *Evangeline*. Each time Miss May came to the end of a section, Caroline was hopelessly torn. She wanted the story to go on and on, but at the same time she longed for it to end. Evangeline spent her whole life searching for Gabriel. When at last she found him, they were both very old, and Gabriel was on his deathbed. They had only a moment together before Gabriel passed on, but it was a joyful reunion. The poet finished the story by going back to the forest of Evangeline's youth:

> *Still stands the forest primeval; but under*
> *the shade of its branches*
> *Dwells another race, with other customs and*
> *language.*

The words made Caroline think again of her own woods. She and her family had a home here, but before they had arrived, there had been others—the family Mother had bought the land from, and before that there had been Indians living in these same woods. Now the family was gone and the Indians were gone. When Caroline looked around her, she could not imagine ever leaving. It seemed as if she would be here forever. It was startling to think that hundreds of years from now, there would be others walking among these same trees and along the banks of this river. It made the world seem very strange and old. And it made Caroline feel like she was seeing everything with new eyes.

For days after Miss May had finished reading the poem, Caroline was aware of an ache deep inside when she remembered the poet's lines. She did not understand how mere words could affect her so deeply.

One late Saturday afternoon, when Miss May had come to help gather the eggs hidden in the tall grasses at the edge of the clearing and to shoo the hens into the henhouse for the night, Caroline got up the courage to ask her about it.

"Poets are blessed with the remarkable ability to make what they see and feel seem very real," Miss May said as she bent down to pluck an egg from its hiding place and tuck it carefully into the basket Caroline was carrying. "There is an ancient proverb my father used to quote," Miss May continued, and her eyes took on the faraway look Caroline had noticed before. "The proverb says that there is 'no more sword to be feared than the learned pen.' Do you know what that means?" She stopped, and now her gray eyes were watching Caroline.

Caroline thought for a moment. "I guess it

means that things that people write can be more frightening than a weapon like a sword," she said slowly.

Miss May gave a nod of her head. "Yes, more frightening and more powerful. Sometimes words can be stronger than any physical weapon."

"But how can that be so?" Caroline asked. "Swords are made of steel."

"True," Miss May replied. "But words can be just as imperishable. Think of our country's beginnings. Our founding fathers knew how important it was to put pen to paper and write down a Declaration of Independence from British rule. The words themselves were just as deadly as any bullet fired in the war to secure our freedom."

Caroline instantly thought of the stirring words she had memorized long ago. She loved to hear the Declaration of Independence when it was read at Glorious Fourth celebrations. It always made her heart beat faster inside her chest.

As she checked to see that the hens were on

their roosts and that the henhouse door was latched, Caroline remained quiet, pondering all that Miss May had said.

"I can tell that you have a serious and thoughtful manner," Miss May said as they walked back to the house. "You remind me a little of myself when I was your age."

Caroline glanced up quickly, returning Miss May's smile. It gave her a warm feeling to know that Miss May thought of her in a special way.

When they reached the kitchen, Martha and Eliza were already setting the table, and Pa and the boys were in from their chores.

"I reckon we're in for a heap of snow this winter," Pa was saying.

"How do you know?" Thomas asked.

"Here," Pa said, opening his large hand. They all gathered around. Pa was holding a hickory nut that he had cracked open. "See the shell?" he asked, and Thomas nodded. "It's thicker than usual. That means a good deal of snow before the winter's through."

"But how does the hickory nut know?"

Eliza asked, and Pa shrugged.

"I don't know how it knows, but it does," he said.

Caroline noticed that lines had formed across Mother's brow. Pa had noticed too. "Now don't worry, Charlotte," he said. "We'll be ready for Old Man Winter long before he shows his face. And you know the old saying as well as I do: 'A year of snow, a year of plenty.'"

Caroline glanced at Miss May, wondering what she would think of Pa's old sayings and his ways of predicting weather.

"May I see the hickory nut too?" Miss May asked. She rolled the nut around in her palm, looking at it with bright, curious eyes; then she turned to Pa. "Did you learn such things from your father?"

"Some," Pa replied. "But my father passed on when I was a young'un. I learned most of what I know about weather and farming from the Winnebago who used to live in these parts."

"How very interesting," Miss May said, and then her eyes took on the faraway look again.

"My father believed we could learn much from the natives who lived here before we settled these shores."

"Your father sounds like he was a wise man," Pa said.

Miss May smiled. "He was," she said.

Now that Pa had said it was time to prepare for winter, every waking moment was filled. The very next day Pa and the boys began to hunt and fish. They came home from the river with buckets of blue gill and pumpkin seed and pickerel and shiners. They came home from the woods with two large deer. For many days, before and after school, Caroline and Martha and Eliza were busy helping Mother with the smoking and the salting so the meat and fish would last through the cold months.

Miss May insisted on helping when she was not preparing for class or writing with her pretty pearl-handled pen in the little day journal she kept. Since she had always lived in a city, where she could buy what she needed from stores, she had never had to prepare for the coming winter. She was amazed at how much work there was to do.

One Saturday, after Pa and the boys had butchered Henry's hog, Caroline and Martha showed Miss May how they made candles from the lard. Candles were made by boiling the fat from the pig all day in a kettle with water. After the water had boiled away, the dirt had to be skimmed off the top. What was left was called tallow.

"Now we dip the wicks into the tallow," Caroline told Miss May.

The wicks were made out of pieces of hemp that the girls had been twisting after supper each night during the past week. Caroline usually did not like dipping candles, because it took hours and hours of dipping the wicks up and down into the hot tallow until the candles grew fat enough. But with Miss May there the chore did not seem so tedious. Miss May was so interested in everything, it made the time pass more quickly.

The next Saturday, Mother and the girls showed Miss May how they made soap. Caroline was not sure which she liked least—making soap or making candles. Both chores were messy and took up much of the day. For hours Caroline took turns with Martha and Eliza, stirring the lye Mother had made from ashes in a big kettle. Then they poured in the lard left over from the week before. When the liquid finally thickened, Mother ladled it into stone crocks. One crock would always be kept by the washbasin in the lean-to.

"My goodness," Miss May said. "How do you know how much to make?"

"Twelve pounds of fat and a barrel of ashes make forty pounds of soap—enough for the whole year," Mother said.

Finally, on the last Saturday of the month, Pa said it was time to thresh the wheat that had been sitting in the barn. The boys began early in the morning. They spread the bundles of wheat on wooden pallets Pa had set in the middle of the barn. Then they beat the heads of the wheat with flails. The flails were two sticks that had been joined together by leather hinges. The boys swung the handle, and the flail whipped down and pounded the wheat heads, shaking the husks free.

All morning they worked. By afternoon the floor of the barn was covered in heaps of husks. Now the good part of the wheat, the kernels, must be separated from the outer skin of the wheat, the chaff. Separating the kernels from the chaff was called winnowing, and that was something Caroline and Martha and Eliza could help with. Miss May said she would help too.

Pa handed out the wooden trays he had made out of old crates. Caroline showed Miss May how to hold the tray flat while the boys shoveled wheat from the barn floor into it. Then Caroline showed how to gently shake the tray up and down so that the light chaff would be blown away. Then the heavier kernels could be poured onto a clean sheet that had been spread on the ground.

Caroline did not tell Miss May, but she did not like winnowing. The trays were heavy, and Caroline quickly grew tired of shaking them again and again. Even when they tied hand-kerchiefs around their faces to protect their

noses and mouths, it was still dusty. Pa told them to chew some wheat gum so they would not be so thirsty. The nutty-tasting wheat gum would make their mouths water even when there was so much dust in the air.

It was long past dark when they finally finished the winnowing. Caroline felt tired and dirty. There was wheat dust worked into every crease of her dress, and she could feel the wheat dust trickling down her back and front.

"I itch all over!" Eliza said.

"So do I," Caroline said, though she knew she shouldn't complain back.

But when Henry shouted, "Ten sacks of grain!" Caroline forgot about being gritty and worn out.

"First thing Monday morning, we'll haul the sacks to the mill," Pa said. "I reckon we'll have wheat for the year, and some extra."

And indeed there was extra. When Caroline came home from school on Monday, Mother's face was bright and she was humming a merry tune.

"Your pa got a fair price for the wheat," she

said, laughing. "A very fair price."

Caroline felt glad down to her very bones. They had never had such a good year. She thought of Pa's saying, "A year of snow, a year of plenty." But now it was backward because they were having their year of plenty first, before the snow.

Now that the wheat flour was packed away in barrels in the pantry, and the leftover straw was in the hayloft for the animals, it was time to see to the garden. Caroline expected that they would be kept home from school for the harvest. But Pa said that the Ingalls boys were still willing to trade work.

"They'll come here in the morning, and we'll head to their place come afternoon," Pa explained.

For a whole week when Caroline came home from school, the kitchen was filled with baskets and sacks of potatoes and turnips, beets and onions, peppers and pumpkins and squash. And for supper each night there was hulled corn and vegetable stew and pumpkin pie. In the evenings the girls sat in the kitchen making pepper and onion braids to hang from the rafters in the pantry. Sometimes while they worked, Miss May read to them from the periodicals she had brought.

At last every single vegetable had been picked and stored away. The shelves in the pantry were full. There were even two whole shelves lined with jars of golden honey. Thomas and Pa had spent an entire day smoking out the bees from the skeps and filling up as many jars as they could. They had left two of the skeps alone, though, so that there would be honey again next year.

One night at supper as they ate some of the good honey and bread, Pa said, "Best honey I've tasted in these parts." He gave a quick nod and casually continued, "Fact is, if I were a betting man, which I am not, I might wager that this here honey could take a prize at a fair."

Mother's eyes were wide. "Why, Frederick," she began, but then seemed at a loss for words. Mother never approved of betting, and Pa had never spoken this way before. Pa cocked his head, and his eyes were merry.

"Seems there's to be a fair hereabouts," he said. "Fact is, it's to be the first State Fair in the state of Wisconsin. I was figuring, well, seeing as how we've got the harvest in in good time, we might take a peek at the fair."

There was a moment of silence. Caroline stared at Pa. She was not sure she had heard him correctly. When she quickly glanced around the table, she could tell her brothers and sisters were all confused as well.

Finally Pa cleared his throat and said, "Well, if none of you wants to go—"

Then there was an explosion of sound.

"Oh yes, Pa! When do we leave? Where is it?" everyone cried at once. Finally Mother found her voice and quieted them all down. Pa told them that the fair was in Janesville and that they would be leaving very early on Friday morning.

Caroline glanced at Miss May. "We have school on Friday," she said.

But Miss May surprised them all. She explained that Mr. Kellogg had already spoken to her about the fair. Since it was the very first state fair, the school board had decided that school should be closed so that all the students would have the opportunity to attend.

Caroline tried to imagine what it would be like at the fair, but she could not. She knew she must be patient and wait for Friday.

State Fair

The week seemed to pass very slowly, but at last Friday arrived. Very early in the morning, before the sun had risen, they set out for the fair dressed in their Sunday best. Mother and Miss May sat on the wagon seat beside Pa, and Caroline and her brothers and sisters sat in back. The air was frosty, but they had quilts and bearskins to snuggle into. They also had the potatoes Mother had heated in the oven to keep in their pockets, so their hands would stay warm.

Packed neatly in one corner of the wagon were the things they were taking to show at the fair. Thomas had packed one of his jars of honey, and Martha had brought one of the straw baskets she had woven after the threshing was done. Caroline and Eliza had both brought the samplers they had made for the new house. Mother had wrapped up one of her pumpkin pies and one of her cranberry pies along with the food she had made for the journey.

Joseph and Henry had not brought anything, but Pa said they would have a chance to win a prize just the same. "There are all kinds of contests, I hear. Plowing and cutting. Even clearing timber. You might come home with a ribbon yet."

Caroline saw her brothers' eyes light up. They were always racing each other at their chores anyway. Now they would have a chance to test their skills against boys from all over the state.

Pa said it would take them all morning to get to Janesville. They would spend the afternoon taking in the sights of the fair, and then they would sleep overnight in the wagon. They would attend the fair again on Saturday morning, and then they would start back Saturday afternoon.

Caroline could hardly believe they would be gone so long. She thought of all the chores they would miss. But Pa and Mother did not seem worried. They said that Wolf would keep any prowlers away, and Mr. Graylick would come by to see to the chickens and the cows. Mr. Graylick and Jacob would not be going to the fair.

When they emerged from the woods, they had to wait before turning onto the Territorial Road because the way was so crowded with people and wagons.

"Are all these folks going to the fair?" Thomas asked in wonder.

"I reckon so," Pa said, nodding his head.

There were lots of men and women and children dressed for Sunday, riding wagons, walking, or hauling carts with pigs and sheep and chickens. Horses went trotting by, and cattle ambled along. There were sheepdogs darting here and there, following their masters. Caroline almost felt they did not need to go to Janesville. It was enough to sit and watch the parade. She was just wondering if Pa would ever be able to find a place in the line of travelers when a friendly voice called out, "Pull in right in front of us, neighbor, and a good morning to you all."

It was Mr. Ingalls. He was driving a handsome team of oxen. Beside him on the high wagon seat sat Mrs. Ingalls, holding baby George on her lap. Lydia and Polly and Docia were sitting in the back with their small brother Hiram. They waved and called out "Good morning!" as Pa called "Giddap!" to get Slow and Ready moving.

Charlie and Jamie were walking alongside the wagon, and when Henry saw this, he asked if he and Joseph and Thomas might do the same.

"Don't see why not," Pa said. "As crowded as this road be, a body might get to Janesville a sight quicker on foot."

After the boys had hopped down, Caroline heard Henry ask where Peter was.

"He drew the short straw," Jamie said, and Caroline wondered what he meant until Charlie explained that he and Peter had drawn straws to see who would get to go to the fair and who would have to stay to look after the place. Caroline was glad that Mr. Graylick had offered to help out and that all her brothers could go.

Now that they were really on their way, Caroline longed to be at the fair in a hurry, but all that morning, the wagon wheels creaked slowly along. Besides being crowded with people, the road itself was full of ruts and dips and bumps. Sometimes there were planks or logs laid across the worst parts of the road, but most of the time the oxen had to pull the wagon over very rough terrain. A few years before, folks had talked about laying down a plank road over this route, but the idea had never taken off. Plank roads were expensive to build and maintain, Pa said.

Caroline grew tired of the constant jolting, but she was glad to be traveling with the Ingallses. It passed the time to turn and wave to Lydia and Polly and Docia. And later in the morning Mother said the girls might walk alongside the wagon with the boys.

"But just for a little ways," Mother said.

It felt good to stretch their legs. The girls walked, but the boys ran up and down the road, racing one another. Together they all joked and laughed and sang. Charlie sang a new song his family had heard as they had come west. It was about the railroad:

> *"Through the mould and through the clay,*
> *Through the corn and through the hay,*
> *By the margin of the lake,*
> *O'er the river, through the brake,*
> *O'er the bleak and dreary moor,*
> *On we hie with screech and roar!"*

Quickly Caroline and the others learned the words and sang them louder and louder until they came to the jolly refrain:

"Dash along!
  Slash along!
   Crash along!
    Flash along
     Oh! with a jump
     And a bump
     And a roll
Hies the fire-fiend to its destined goal!"

When they got to the final verse, they would wait a moment and then start it up again. It was a good traveling song, full of might and muscle. The grown-ups joined in, and Caroline noticed that Mr. Ingalls had a fine deep voice. As they sang, Caroline wondered what it would be like to see a real live locomotive dashing and crashing through the countryside. She had seen pictures of the railroad in newspapers, but she had never seen one in person. It was hard to imagine something that could move so straight and swiftly. Joseph and Henry had seen the railroad when they had gone to Watertown with Pa. And Charlie had seen one back east.

"The guy who wrote that song got it right on the money," Charlie said. "Fire-fiend suits it to a T."

An hour before noon, they stopped the wagons alongside the road so they could eat an early dinner and let the animals rest. The boys saw to the oxen, and the girls spread out the quilts and the food each family had brought.

"At last we get to have a visit, even if it *is* in nature's parlor," Mrs. Ingalls said to Mother. To Miss May, she said, "And I have so wanted to make your acquaintance. The girls have never liked school so much."

As they sat eating their cold dinner, Caroline decided she liked Mrs. Ingalls a great deal. She could tell that Mother and Miss May did too. Mrs. Ingalls was bright and cheerful, with soft brown hair framing a round face and kind brown eyes.

Mr. Ingalls was more reserved than his wife. In fact he seemed rather severe as he sat quietly in his good black suit and black hat. His thick dark hair already had two streaks of white in it and was combed neatly back. His black beard reached to his collar. But Caroline soon discovered that his sharp blue eyes could suddenly twinkle at some merriment just like Charlie's.

Caroline decided that the Ingallses were a jolly family, all in all. They were quick to laugh and joke with one another, and they were cheerful among new friends. The trip to the fair was even more of an adventure now that there were friends to share it with.

When the wagons began to roll again, both Mother and Mrs. Ingalls were in agreement. Everyone—even the boys—must ride the final stretch to Janesville.

"Otherwise you will be too worn out to enjoy yourselves," Mother said firmly.

So for the rest of the trip Caroline sat squashed in between Joseph and Martha, watching quietly as fields and houses and trees rolled by. Everywhere she looked, the world was drenched in color. There was the blue sky overhead, and the vibrant reds and yellows of the trees lining the road. The fields were a rich brown, having been turned over for the winter.

The grass was still green in places, but mostly it had faded into a soft golden color. They passed little farms just like their own with log cabins or plain plank houses. Sometimes small girls and boys waved to them from inside fences made of stone or split rails.

At last, when Caroline had nearly dozed off from the steady rocking of the wagon wheels, Pa announced that they had arrived. Caroline's eyes popped open, and she saw something striped blue and white up ahead. It was a tent, the largest tent she had ever seen, much larger than any house. The roof of the tent sloped up into five pointed peaks, and at the top of each peak a blue flag rippled in the breeze. The great tent was inside a circle of white fence.

"That's the fairgrounds," Pa said.

Caroline looked around. She saw a large sign that said

Wisconsin Agricultural State Fair

in bold letters. Beyond the sign there were smaller tents and makeshift booths and stands.

There were long sheds with slanting roofs. Great crowds of people were pouring in and out of the fairgrounds. Everywhere, people were talking and shouting and laughing. Somewhere a band played, and the music was bright and lively. It was like the Glorious Fourth celebrations Caroline had attended back in Brookfield, but it was much bigger.

Pa and Mr. Ingalls turned their wagons away from the fairgrounds into a large flat field where many other wagons were stopped. The boys hurried to give the oxen water and oats and to put them on picket lines. Caroline slowly climbed out of the wagon. Her legs were stiff from sitting so long.

"What do we do now?" Charlie asked, rubbing his hands together. He looked as if he were about to pounce on something.

"No use keeping these boys in harness, is there, Holbrook?" Mr. Ingalls asked. His mouth was a straight line, but his blue eyes were merry.

"I reckon it would be near impossible," Pa replied.

And so the boys—all except for little Hiram and baby George, of course—were allowed to go off on their own after Mother made Joseph promise to keep a strict eye on Thomas and Jamie. Mr. Ingalls and Pa led Mother and Mrs. Ingalls and Miss May and the rest of the children slowly through the swirl of fairgoers.

"I didn't know there would be so very many people," Eliza said in a timid voice as she clutched her sampler against her chest and looked around with large eyes.

Caroline reached down to take a firm hold of Eliza's hand. Her own heart was still fluttering very fast, and she realized that she felt just as unsettled as Eliza. At the Glorious Fourth celebrations in Brookfield she had known many of the people. Here they were among strangers. But she screwed up her courage and said to Eliza in a bold voice, "Don't worry. We will not lose each other."

Eliza held more tightly to Caroline's hand, but when she smiled, she seemed to be more at ease.

Once they were inside the fairgrounds, they

headed for the large tent. Caroline noticed a sign along the front of it that read,

Main Exhibition of Domestic Goods.

It seemed very dark inside the tent after they had been so long in the bright sunlight. As Caroline's eyes adjusted to the dim light, she saw that there were little lanterns hanging from poles that crisscrossed the tent's ceiling, and long tables had been set up stretching the length of the floor.

Mr. Ingalls and Pa stopped to talk to a man with a white beard and a wide smile on his round, ruddy face. His large belly was barely held inside a red-and-black-striped vest. A badge pinned to his chest said JUDGE. He pointed them in the direction of a group of tables where several ladies were helping to organize things.

"Please write your name and place of residence on one of these cards and pin it to your entry," one of the ladies said.

"You do it," Martha said to Caroline when it

was their turn. "Your writing is better than mine."

So Caroline took the quill pen and carefully wrote on Martha's card and then Eliza's. Then she wrote on her own:

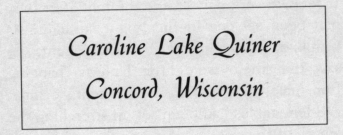

Caroline Lake Quiner
Concord, Wisconsin

Caroline looked at the cards on the sampler table. There were contestants from all over the state. It felt very important to put her sampler beside another made by a Mavis Perkins from Kenosha.

After that they went to the far side of the tent, where the tables were laden with all kinds of delicious-looking pies. Mrs. Ingalls had made an apple pie and a custard pie. She placed hers beside Mother's.

"I bet Henry wouldn't mind being a judge at this contest," Martha said.

"What do they do with all the pies after the judge has had a taste?" Eliza asked.

Pa nodded toward a sign that said:

Pay a Nickel – All You Can Eat.

Caroline looked around. There were a lot of pies. But a nickel was a lot of money.

Somehow Pa seemed to sense what she was thinking. "It's not just for the pie," he explained. "Come five o'clock, there will be all kinds of good things to eat."

Caroline and Martha and Eliza looked at one another. They knew Mother had packed extra food for the journey, but they had assumed they would be eating it together at the wagon. Did Pa mean that they would be paying a nickel apiece to eat here in the big tent? They did not dare ask.

"Let's wait and see," Martha whispered to Caroline.

Now Pa and Mr. Ingalls set off to look at the livestock and the displays of farm implements and to talk with other farmers. The fair was not just about games and contests. It was also a chance for men to meet together and talk about new ideas for farming.

"I wonder if Mr. McCormick is here with his reaper," Mr. Ingalls said as they set off.

Mother and Mrs. Ingalls and Miss May strolled among the tables, the girls following behind with Hiram and baby George in tow. They looked at all the beautiful quilts and embroidery and needlepoint and woolwork and baskets and brooms. There were handsome lamp mats and fine table spreads and colorful rolls of woven cloth.

"When will they give out ribbons?" Eliza asked.

"Not until tomorrow," Mother replied.

Caroline was strolling beside Miss May when she stopped at the printers' table. Printers from all over were displaying printed cards and books and pamphlets. There were books of poetry and everyday sayings, and there were day journals like Miss May's. Caroline admired one of the day journals that was particularly pretty. It had a rose-colored marbled cover, and inside, the months of the year were printed in lovely golden letters.

"Would you be interested in owning a day journal, Caroline?" Miss May asked.

"Oh, yes," Caroline said. However, after a moment she added, "But I'm not sure what I would write in one." She was thinking of how often Miss May wrote in hers during recess at school or after supper at home.

"Well," Miss May said, "as I have told you in school, you are a good writer, Caroline, and you seem to share my interest in words. I think you would find much to write about."

Caroline blushed a little. "Thank you," she said.

Miss May continued as they walked along. "I myself like to jot down little thoughts that come to me during the day. Or I jot down something new that I have seen or experienced. That way, in later years, when my memory is not as trustworthy, I can go back and relive things that have happened in my life."

Imperishable, Caroline thought, remembering their discussion a few weeks before. Words could make memories imperishable.

"Do you write down the bad things as well as the good?" Caroline asked.

"Sometimes," Miss May answered.

Now Caroline thought of the day, years before, when they had learned Father was not ever coming back, and of all the days right after that, when things had been so difficult for the family. She was not sure she would want to remember the hard times.

"Most of the time I write down the good things," Miss May said. "Take boarding with your family, for instance. I have had many wonderful moments, which I will look back on fondly when I am no longer here."

They said no more, but Caroline had a warm feeling inside, as she always did when talking with Miss May. It felt grown-up, and she knew that Miss May understood her.

After they had finished looking at all the tables, Mother and Mrs. Ingalls said that the girls might walk around the fairgrounds on their own as long as they promised to stay together and act like little ladies.

"You must be back at this exact spot by four o'clock," Mrs. Ingalls added.

"Yes, ma'am," they all sang.

"And remember girls," Mother said more quietly, taking Caroline and Martha and Eliza aside. "If you decide to spend your pennies, do so wisely."

Caroline felt inside the pocket of her skirt. Five pennies were tucked there, and she knew that Martha had five pennies as well. They had saved them from the last five Christmases. Eliza only had three pennies. Caroline wondered if they were supposed to save them for supper. She did not think so. Otherwise Mother would have said.

"Let's go! Let's go!" Docia squealed, pulling on Lydia's and Polly's hands.

Caroline followed the girls out into the sunlight again. They passed slowly along rows of booths and stands and small tents decorated with colorful signs and banners. In front of many of the booths, men in dapper suits and tall top hats were shouting to the crowd.

"Step right up, step right up!"

"Don't be shy! Everybody's a winner."

"Only a nickel for the chance of a lifetime."

The girls stopped to watch some boys toss wooden rings over stakes in the ground to try to win caramel apples. Then they watched as a man who called himself Doctor All-Good poured a thick black liquid over another man's head. The sign over the booth said:

DOCTOR ALL-GOOD'S AMAZING HAIR TONIC
For the Preservation, Beauty, Growth, and Restoration of the Hair

---

"Newly improved!" Doctor All-Good was shouting. "This is my new and improved liquid hair dye. This dye, when strictly applied, will immediately change the hair from any other color to a beautiful black, without injury to the skin."

When Dr. All-Good was finished applying the dye, he threw up his hands and scanned the crowd. He smiled all the while, showing a gold tooth that glinted in the sun.

"Wait and see, ladies and gentlemen, boys

and girls. It takes only a moment, my friends, and the gray is gone as if by magic. A perfect item for Ma and Pa and Granny alike. Takes years off the looks of any man or woman."

Now the doctor dunked the man's head into a bucket of water. The poor man came up spluttering, but Dr. All-Good quickly toweled him off and ran a comb through his hair. Sure enough, the man's locks were as black as a crow's feathers.

"But what if your hair wasn't black to begin with?" Martha said under her breath. Caroline and Eliza began to giggle, and the giggling spread to Lydia and Polly and Docia. They saw Dr. All-Good looking sternly in their direction and they fled, giggling, to the next booth, where another doctor was hawking a tonic to purify the blood.

"None of us are sick or gray," Polly said, so they moved on to another booth, which was not a booth exactly. It was like a little house on wheels. A neat little house that had been painted a bright red, with curtained windows along the sides. The wheels had been painted a cheerful yellow. Along one side of the house there was a sign that read in bold letters,

DAGUERREOTYPE SALOON

And under that there was a banner that read,

**Secure the shadow ere the substance fade,
Let Nature imitate what Nature made!**

In front of the little house a man in a handsome brown-and-white-striped suit was standing beside a strange contraption like nothing Caroline had ever seen. It was a small black box that stood on three long stiltlike legs. A black curtain hung from one side of the box.

The man tipped his hat at the crowd and began to speak. "Ladies and gentleman, girls and boys, my name is Winston Dunbar, and I have had the singular pleasure of traveling across this great land of ours, spreading joy and comfort to those who will but take a few moments of their time to ensure that their loved ones have a token, a memento, to cherish when they themselves have left this fair plain."

The crowd began to grow, and Mr. Dunbar spoke louder.

"No one knows, my friends, when our journey here is at an end. Therefore I urge each and every one of you to ensure that you leave something behind. And what can be more appropriate than a daguerreotype? A perfect likeness of yourself in the prime of health."

"How long does it take to make one of them likenesses?" someone shouted from the crowd.

"It takes but a few moments of your time, my good man," Mr. Dunbar said. "Five short minutes for the exposure to be made. Another five minutes for the process to be complete."

A murmur went through the crowd. "How much does it cost?" a man standing near Caroline shouted.

"One dollar, my friend," Mr. Dunbar replied. "Only one dollar to give your sweetheart something to keep you near and dear."

"Ain't got no sweetheart," the man mumbled, and several people in the crowd guffawed. "And even if I did, a dollar's a lot of money."

"But well worth it, I assure you," Mr. Dunbar said in his smooth voice. "Do not take my word alone," he continued. "Please, step into my gallery and feast your eyes on what the new London process can accomplish. You shall be astounded, I assure you."

Mr. Dunbar led the crowd to the back of the little house, where a velvet curtain hung over a small door. "The gallery will accommodate only six bodies at a time," he called. "And so I must ask you all to be patient."

Caroline and her sisters and friends were near the front of the line, so they had to wait just a little while. As soon as she stepped inside, Caroline felt she had entered another world. All about her, tiny faces stared out from delicate little golden frames or larger, handsome frames made of silver and velvet. The walls themselves were papered in a rich red-and-gold print, and the ceiling was not a ceiling at all, but a large window of glass. There was a dainty settee of red velvet in one corner.

It was a unique little place. But best of all were those daguerreotypes. Caroline stood breathless, peering from one to the other. There were girls her age, dressed in the finest silk and lace, and boys in tailored suits. There were tiny babies in long white linen gowns. There were couples and whole families standing side by side.

"They look awfully grim," Lydia whispered.

But Caroline thought they looked stately. She did not want to leave the little room with all the faces to study, but she knew others were waiting their turn.

When they stepped outside again, a young married couple had decided to have their image taken, and so Mr. Dunbar was setting the scene. Caroline saw that on the other side of the little house, a great curtain of gray velvet hung from the top of the wagon and fell in folds along the ground in a kind of train. On

top of the train sat a velvet chair and an ornate stand with a vase of peacock feathers.

Mr. Dunbar had the young lady sit on the velvet chairs. He positioned the gentleman directly behind her with his hand resting on her shoulder.

"Please settle yourselves into a comfortable position," Mr. Dunbar said. He then took a kind of clamp that was attached to the back of the chair and placed it so that it cradled the back of the young lady's head.

"I assure you this is not some kind of torture device," Mr. Dunbar joked. "It is to help you maintain your position in comfort. I must remind you both that you must remain perfectly still for the full five minutes."

After Mr. Dunbar had the young lady secured, he set another tall clamp behind the gentleman's head. Several people in the crowd laughed out loud.

"Looks like you're harnessing them up like oxen in a yoke," someone joked.

The young couple turned red and looked as if they were thinking better of having their image taken. But it was too late now. They were stuck in place.

Mr. Dunbar brought around the little black box on stilts and positioned it several feet in front of the couple. "I remind you that you must maintain a relaxed facial expression," he said. "Do not attempt to smile, for you will not be able to hold your lips in that position for long. Please simply look natural."

Caroline thought the couple looked more alarmed than relaxed, but Mr. Dunbar seemed satisfied. He ducked under the long black curtain and said, "Now!"

Some boys in the crowd began calling out, trying to get the couple to laugh. Caroline thought she saw the lady twitch. She thought that she would like to have a daguerreotype made, but not in front of so many people.

"Let's go," Martha said.

Reluctantly Caroline followed her little group to the next booth. She would have liked to stay to see the image, but it was hard to wait ten whole minutes when there was so much to see and do.

At the next booth a man was selling hot apple cider and squares of warm gingerbread.

"I'm thirsty," Eliza said. "And I'm hungry too."

The cider cost one penny and the ginger-bread cost two. Caroline looked at the booth. Suddenly it seemed a long time since they had eaten their dinner by the side of the road.

Caroline and Martha and Eliza decided that they would each put one penny in—then they could share one cup of cider and one piece of gingerbread. Lydia and Polly and Docia decided to do the same. After they had handed over their pennies, they waited as the man poured out two cups of cider from a large crock that was heating over a little cookstove. Then he cut two squares of gingerbread.

The girls stood beside the booth, taking turns sipping from the tin cups and biting into the gingerbread. The cider was wonderfully tangy, and the gingerbread was sweet.

After they had handed their cups back to the man in the booth, they followed the sound of music until they were standing in front of a small platform gaily decorated with banners in red, white, and blue. A brass band was playing a rousing march. The girls began to move their feet and clap their hands to the music, along with the rest of the onlookers. They stayed to listen to one song and then another, until it was nearly four o'clock.

"We have to hurry!" Martha urged, and they wound their way back toward the main tent.

Inside, Pa and Mr. Ingalls and the boys were already there with Mrs. Ingalls and Miss May. Caroline noticed that Mother was smiling her brightest smile as she spoke to a smartly dressed couple. As Caroline came closer, Mother looked up and said, "Here they are." The man turned, and Caroline was staring into familiar dark eyes that crinkled in the corners.

"Are you girls too big to give your old friend a hug?" the man asked, and suddenly Caroline and Eliza and even Martha were all nearly shouting, "Mr. Ben! Mr. Ben!"

Two Charlies

Mr. Ben Carpenter bent down to fold Caroline and Martha and Eliza into a great, warm embrace. Then he stepped back so that Mrs. Carpenter could give them a proper greeting as well.

"How wonderful to see you!" Mrs. Carpenter said.

The Carpenters had been their good friends in Brookfield. Mr. Ben, as the children called him, had helped the family move to Concord and had stayed several weeks to help them settle in. But Caroline and her family had not seen the Carpenters since then.

"Are these really my pretty girls who left us three years ago?" Mr. Carpenter asked, shaking his head. "Why, they are all grown up!"

Caroline realized that she had indeed grown since she had seen Mr. Ben last. She did not need to raise her chin nearly so high to smile into his cheerful face.

"They're not the only ones who've done some growing," Henry spoke up. "Lookee here." He stepped aside to reveal a tall young man who wore a half grin on his handsome face. "Martha, don't you recognize Charlie?"

Caroline could hardly believe the striking young man in front of her was Charlie Carpenter. She could tell Martha could hardly believe it either. Martha's cheeks turned a bright pink, and a hand fluttered up to straighten her bonnet. Caroline knew that Martha had always been sweet on Charlie Carpenter.

Charlie pushed a lock of black hair out of his eyes and in a deep voice greeted Caroline and Eliza. Then he turned and said, "Hello,

Miss Martha," just like he used to do back in
Brookfield. His dark eyes were laughing, and
Martha let out a small laugh herself. Her
cheeks were still pink, but Caroline thought
she looked very pretty under her bonnet.

"Hello, Charlie," Martha said in a quiet
voice, her eyes sparkling.

"Just think!" Mr. Ben was saying. "In this
great big jumble of folks, we run into our old
friends."

"I can hardly believe it myself," Mother
said. "I have missed your company so."

"And we have sorely missed yours, Charlotte," Mrs. Carpenter replied.

Just then Pa stepped forward and cleared his
throat. "I do not mean to break up this happy
reunion, but the judges are almost finished
judging the pies."

They looked up in time to see the judge
from earlier that day walking down the aisle.

"Now I see why he has such a big belly,"
Eliza whispered, and Caroline couldn't help
but let out a little giggle.

They all held their breath and watched as

the judge placed a yellow ribbon on Mother's pumpkin pie and another on Mrs. Ingalls' apple pie. The ribbons had HONORABLE MENTION written in gold lettering.

"I would have given you a blue ribbon for sure," Mr. Ben said to Mother. "I certainly do miss your good cooking, Charlotte."

But Mother was pleased as she fingered her ribbon, and so was Mrs. Ingalls. Mrs. Carpenter had not brought any pies. She had brought her woolwork, which would be judged the next day.

"Looks like it's eating time," Mr. Ben said, and sure enough, Caroline saw what she had not noticed before: Beyond the pie tables there were more tables on which was spread a huge feast.

"Are you staying for supper?" Mother asked, and Mr. Carpenter said he would not miss it for the world. "I'd pay a nickel just to eat the rest of that pumpkin pie of yours," he said.

Several men went through the crowd carrying baskets. One of them was calling out, "It's an honor system, ladies and gentlemen. But please be aware that your money goes to help in the organizing of a second state fair next year."

Mr. Ingalls counted out his money and dropped it in. Caroline was still not sure if they were staying until she saw Pa reach into his pocket and count out eight nickels. Then he dropped the coins into the basket.

"Are we really eating here?" Caroline asked, and Mother smiled and answered, "Yes, Caroline."

"You mean we can eat anything we want?" Henry asked, and Mother again answered yes. "Does that mean we could only eat pie if we wanted?" Henry wanted to know.

Caroline saw Pa's lips twitch in amusement. "Yes, but I would hope you'd decide to eat more than just pie, young man."

"Better step up," Mr. Ben said. "With this crowd, you might end up with empty plates."

"I am quite sure Henry would never let that happen," Mother said, and they all laughed and went forward to sample that wonderful food.

There were boiled hams and platters of roast beef and roast chickens and turkeys. Next to that were bowls of dressing and potatoes and gravy and mashed turnips and beans and onions. There were pickles and preserves and jellies. On one table there were many different kinds of bread: rye bread and hot biscuits and corn bread and corn cakes and salt-rising bread and Swedish crackers.

Caroline took a tin plate from a tall stack nearby and went with Polly to the large, over-flowing tables.

"Have you ever seen so much food in your entire life?" Polly asked.

Caroline shook her head. "No, never."

"I don't know what to choose—it all looks so good," Polly said.

"I guess we could take a little bit of every-thing," Caroline suggested, and that's just what they did. When their plates were full, they went outside to the tables Pa and Mr. Ingalls and Mr. Ben had found for them.

The light was fading from the sky, but there were little tin lanterns with tiny holes poked in them hanging from stakes driven into the ground.

The Carpenters sat with Caroline and her family and Miss May at one long table while the Ingallses sat at the other. There was a lot to talk about, but everyone was busy eating. Caroline and Polly could not think of going back for seconds, but all the boys had third helpings and even fourths.

"Aren't you fellows going to save room for pie?" Mr. Ben asked teasingly.

"There's room enough yet," Charlie Carpenter answered, patting his belly and turning to wink at Martha. Caroline couldn't think where all that food went, because Charlie was still as thin as a split rail.

After sharing a slice of pie with Eliza, Caroline knew she could eat no more. She had never been so full in her life. She did not think she could move, but after a time she stood and followed the other girls and ladies when Mother said they must help clean up. In another large tent washtubs were set up, and women and girls were tying on makeshift aprons over their good clothes. Mother and Mrs. Carpenter chatted as they washed dishes.

"Oh, you would not recognize Brookfield now, Charlotte," Mrs. Carpenter said. "It is such a bustling town. Ben can hardly stand it. He keeps talking of taking a claim farther west. And of course Charlie is all for it. But I must say, I've grown quite accustomed to living the civilized life."

Mother asked after some of the friends they had left behind. Caroline's ears pricked up when she heard that Mr. Short had married a nice widow from Waukesha. Anna Short had been her best friend in Brookfield. Caroline hoped that Anna liked her new ma.

When at last all the many dishes and platters and crocks had been washed and dried, Caroline's family and the Ingallses and Carpenters made their way out of the fairgrounds. The Carpenters were not camping in the field. They were staying in a hotel in town. But Mr. Ben said they would stay to chat awhile. And so the boys hurried to find kindling to build a fire, while the girls helped to bring the quilts and bearskins out and lay them on the ground.

All across the field other families were doing the same. Bonfires dotted the dark plain, mirroring the starry sky above. The night air was cold, but once the fire was roaring, Caroline felt warm. She sat next to Polly listening to the voices around her. There were the muffled voices of strangers coming out of the dark, from the wagons nearby, and there were the louder, familiar voices close by.

Henry and Joseph were telling Mr. Ben about the changes that had been made on the farm since he had seen it last. Mother and Mrs. Carpenter were still chatting of Brookfield. Mrs. Ingalls was talking with Miss May about New York. Pa and Mr. Ingalls sat discussing the new inventions they had seen that day. Mr. McCormick had not been showing his famous reaper. But another fellow named Esterly from Heart Prairie was showing the one he had invented.

"It looked to me to be a fine machine," Mr. Ingalls said. "But I hear the McCormick is all the go."

Docia and Hiram and George had fallen asleep, but Charlie Ingalls was making Lydia and Jamie and Eliza and Thomas laugh as he threw shadow pictures against one side of the wagon. After a while Henry came to join him.

"Goose! Rabbit! Bird! Dog!" Caroline and Polly called along with the others each time the boys slipped their hands into a new shape.

Caroline noticed that Martha and Charlie Carpenter were sitting close together on a log. They were watching the shadow shapes, but they were having their own quiet conversation. Every once in a while Charlie would say something that made Martha smile, and then he would smile too. Caroline couldn't help but think how pretty her sister looked with the glow from the fire lighting up her face. Suddenly Caroline realized that Martha really was growing up. The thought made her feel a little lonely.

"Hey, now we have two Charlies." Henry

spoke up, pointing back and forth between Charlie Ingalls and Charlie Carpenter, and forcing Caroline's lonely thoughts out of her head. "How will we know who we're talking about?"

The two Charlies looked at each other.

"I think you should call us Charles the First and Charles the Second, just like the kings," Charlie Carpenter said laughingly.

"But who is the first and who is the second?" Henry wanted to know.

"Well, seeing as how I've known these folks longer, I reckon I should be the first," Charlie Carpenter boldly said.

Charlie Ingalls thought about this for a moment. "Well, all right," he laughed. "Though I'm not sure I like the idea of kings in America."

After that they went back to making shadows until the sound of music came drifting out of the dark. At first it was just a fiddle, but then a few voices joined in.

"Hey, Charles the Second," Henry said. "How about some dueling fiddles?"

"Didn't bring my fiddle along," Charlie

Ingalls said, and Caroline could hear the disappointment in his voice.

As the fiddle played on, Caroline noticed that he seemed to strain toward the sound. The fingers of his left hand twitched at his side, as if he were fingering notes. The unknown fiddler played several familiar tunes, and all around more and more voices were raised in song. Then he played a song Caroline had never heard before. Only one man was singing, and his voice was deep and resonant.

"Oh Shenandoah, I long to hear you.
Way hey, you rolling river.
Oh Shenandoah, I long to hear you.
Away, we're bound away
'Cross the wide Missouri."

Just like the poetry Miss May had read to them, the song with its haunting words and melody made her heart ache, although she did not know exactly why.

"Goodness, how late it is!" Mother said

when the fiddler stopped his playing. The moon was high in the deep black sky. All around, folks began calling good night. The Carpenters said they must be going.

"We'll see you all tomorrow, though," Mr. Ben said.

Now they laid the quilts and bearskins in the wagon bed and under the wagon. Mother and Miss May and Eliza would sleep inside the wagon. Martha and Caroline would lie underneath, and Pa and the boys would sleep near the fire.

"Is it good to see Charles the First?" Caroline whispered when she and Martha were lying close together wrapped in quilts.

Martha let out a little giggle at the name. "Yes," she whispered back. She was quiet for a moment, and then she said, "But he is so awfully handsome now." Her voice sounded worried.

"He is," Caroline replied, and then added quickly, "but I am sure Charlie was thinking the same thing. How awfully pretty you are now."

"Do you think so?" Martha asked timidly.

"Yes, I do," Caroline answered frankly. Martha squeezed her hand under the covers.

Caroline did not think she would sleep, since her head still buzzed with all she had seen and heard that day, but before she knew it, her lids were growing heavy and she was drifting off. In her dreams faces appeared and disappeared and bodies bustled to and fro. Strange men were shouting in voices that seemed quiet at first but grew louder and louder, until Caroline awoke with a start and realized that it was morning and she was in a strange place far from home and it was very cold. All around her there were shouts as the fair started up again. Martha laughed when she saw Caroline's startled face.

"Did you forget where we were?" Martha asked. Caroline nodded, and Martha smiled. "So did I," she said.

Quickly they scrambled out from under the wagon and hurried to warm themselves by the fire. Mother and Mrs. Ingalls were already cooking breakfast.

"It's been a while since I cooked over a fire," Mother was saying.

"Not so long for me," Mrs. Ingalls said. "But Lansford has promised me that we are staying in one place for a while."

Joseph had brought some water from a nearby well, and they all took turns at the bucket washing their hands and faces. Martha asked Caroline if she would braid her hair and pin it up. "You do it so nicely," she said.

"Of course I will," Caroline answered as she started combing Martha's hair.

"Oh, I wish we had brought a change of clothes," Martha said, tugging at her skirt to straighten the hem. For a moment Caroline was surprised. Martha did not care so much about clothes. Then she realized that Martha was thinking of Charlie Carpenter.

"The dress looks as nice as it did yesterday," Caroline said, helping to brush a few strands of grass from the back. "And now your hair is done, and it looks lovely."

"Thank you, Caroline!" Martha breathed.

"Hurry, girls!" Mother called. She and Mrs.

Ingalls were already dishing up the tin plates of fried salt pork and beans and corn bread cooked in the iron skillet.

As soon as they had finished their breakfast and put away the dishes, the Carpenters came walking up. Caroline noticed that they were dressed in the same clothes they had been wearing the day before. She hoped this made Martha feel better.

"Good morning, one and all!" Mr. Ben boomed. "Are you boys ready to show your muscle?"

"Yes sir!" Joseph and Henry and Charlie Ingalls called all together.

"Then let's see who has the gumption this fine morning to bring home a ribbon," Mr. Ben said, and they all headed toward the field where the races would take place.

First there was a plowing contest. Joseph and Henry and both Charlies took their places behind plows that had been placed in a straight line at the edge of the field. Caroline let out a little scream along with the other girls and ladies as a pistol was fired into the air by one of the judges. The long line of plows rushed forward. There was much cheering and clapping from the sidelines as a few plowers moved ahead of the pack. Caroline squealed when she saw that Joseph was one of those in the lead. Henry had fallen a little behind, and so had the two Charlies.

"That's the way!" men were shouting from the crowd. "Put your shoulder into it. We haven't got all day!"

At first it seemed that Joseph might win, but then another man pushed forward and Joseph came in second. Caroline felt a stab of disappointment that her brother had not won first place, but Joseph was beaming when they found him in the crowd. The judge had pinned a red ribbon on his chest, and friends and strangers alike were patting him on the back.

"A job well done," Pa said proudly.

The next competition was cradling. Henry and Joseph and the two Charlies all gave a good show, but they could not win against the larger men. Pa and Mr. Ingalls and Mr. Ben tried their hand at rail splitting and they were a good match, but they did not win any ribbons to bring home either.

After the contests were over, Mother and the other ladies headed back to the main tent. Everyone else went into the sheds where the cows and sheep and pigs and horses were being housed. Here the judges had already awarded prizes. Groups of men crowded the stalls, congratulating the winners.

"Bess is as pretty as any of those," Thomas said, pointing toward the pen that held the calves. Like all the other animals, they had been washed and brushed until their coats shone. The calf that had won was spotted like Bess.

When they came out of the sheds, the grounds were even more crowded. It took a long time to reach the main tent, where Mother and Mrs. Ingalls and Mrs. Carpenter were waiting. The judges had already gone down the tables.

"Congratulations to you, my dears," Mother said, her face beaming. Caroline's heart leaped because at first she thought Mother was speaking to her. But then she realized Mother was looking at Martha and Thomas.

Thomas' honey had gotten a yellow ribbon, but Martha's basket had gotten a red ribbon. Martha had gotten second place! In all the state of Wisconsin, her basket had been the second best.

Martha's face was full of surprise as everyone crowded around to congratulate her. Caroline knew it was not right to be a sore loser, but she could not get the words out to compliment Martha. Her sampler was every bit as good as Martha's basket! She felt her eyes stinging, and she turned and walked toward the table where her sampler sat ribbonless. She saw that Eliza had not won a ribbon, but it did not matter.

Caroline stood for a long time, hiding the tears that had welled up in her eyes, until she realized someone was standing beside her.

She glanced up to see Miss May.

"I think it's a very pretty sampler," Miss May said.

"Thank you," Caroline managed to say. She took the sampler from the table and looked at it. Deep down she knew that the stitches were not as small and straight as they could be. Her mouth opened, and she was suddenly saying something she had never admitted to anyone. "I do not like to sew." Caroline put her hand over her mouth, but then she just had to continue. "You see, Mother was a dressmaker, and she can sew anything. And I want to be good and sew pretty things. But really, I get tired of trying to make the stitches so small and perfect. And the needle pricks your finger and your hands start to ache."

Caroline looked up at Miss May, thinking that the teacher would scold her and tell her that all young ladies should like to sew, but Miss May was not wearing a scolding face. Her large gray eyes held a twinkle and her lips were turned up at the edges.

"We all have our strengths, Caroline," Miss May said. "I myself have never been fond of passing the time with a needle and thread."

Caroline let out a little laugh, but she looked around to make sure no one else had heard. "Oh, please don't tell Mother," she begged.

"Your secret is safe with me," Miss May replied, still smiling.

Now Caroline felt better. She hurried back into the crowd to congratulate Thomas and Martha.

"I'm sorry about your sampler, Caroline," Martha said.

"Me too. But you deserved to win. It's a beautiful basket." And Caroline meant it with all her heart.

It was nearly noon, and that meant it was time to head back to Concord. The Carpenters were staying another night, and Caroline wished they could too. But Mother said they had been gone long enough. Mother kissed Mrs. Carpenter on the cheek and hugged her close.

"This has been such a wonderful surprise," Mother said.

"We must not let so much time pass before our next meeting," Mrs. Carpenter replied. Caroline saw her glance toward Martha, who was talking with her son. Mother caught the look, and they both smiled.

"No, we must not," Mother said.

Mr. Ben enveloped Caroline and her sisters in another great hug. "I am glad to see my girls again," he said. "I know your father would have been proud of you." He tugged Caroline's long braid hanging halfway down her back.

"I guess you're not Little Brown Braid anymore, are you?" he asked.

Caroline felt her eyes well up once more with tears. She could not answer but could only shake her head. It had been the nickname Father had given her long ago, but she had outgrown it. She looked into Mr. Ben's eyes. It had been a long time since she had spoken to anyone outside the family who had known her father. It suddenly made Caroline feel that Father was close by.

Mr. Ben gave the braid another tug, and then the Carpenters were swallowed up in the crowd. Caroline looked to see if Martha was crying, but she was not. Her face glowed and she wore a faraway smile.

"I wish I could give Charlie one of those daguerreotypes of myself," she whispered to Caroline on the way out of the fairgrounds. "That way he wouldn't forget me."

"I am sure he won't forget you," Caroline whispered back.

When they reached the wagons, they ate a quick dinner, and then they all scrambled up into their places. Caroline kept turning to watch as the crowds and the great blue-and-white tent grew smaller and smaller behind them. It was sad to be leaving the fair. Everyone seemed to feel the same. The wagon was quiet as they rolled slowly along behind the Ingallses.

"Mighty quiet back there," Pa said over his shoulder. "Maybe this will perk you all up." He half turned in the seat and handed a small paper bag to Joseph. "There's one for each of you."

Caroline saw Joseph reach into the bag and pull out a red-and-white-striped stick.

"Peppermint candy!" Thomas cried as the bag went from hand to hand. The boys ate theirs right away, but Caroline and Martha and Eliza made theirs last the whole long ride home.

School Ends

It seemed as though the sunny autumn weather had stayed around only long enough for the fair. The very next week a sharp wind blew down from the north, and the days turned gray and very cold.

"Pa knew!" Thomas yelled when they woke up to find a thick snow on the ground.

Pa rubbed a hand along his knee. "I reckon winter is already here," he said. "I feel it in my bones."

Caroline couldn't help but think it was just. They had had their plenty; now they would have their snow.

Each day was colder than the last, and walking to and from school became a chore. Caroline wore five layers of clothing, but the wind pierced through her flannels and extra petticoat and wool dress and coat and shawl as if she were only wearing a summer frock.

Now the older boys came to school, and the one room was very crowded. There were a couple of boys Caroline did not know along with Peter and Joseph and Henry and Charlie and Jacob Graylick. The big boys took turns filling the woodbox and keeping the fire burning in the stove, but even so the room was cold. Miss May always made sure the smallest children stayed closest to the warmth.

Caroline often thought of how Mrs. Spivey had been so sure that a lady teacher could not keep order, especially when there was a room full of big boys. But Miss May had made the new arrivals respect her by being strict but not mean, and by making the lessons interesting. Caroline wished Mrs. Spivey could see how they all got along so well.

On Fridays they continued to have spell-downs. Caroline thought it was exciting now that there were more scholars to compete against. Sometimes it was boys against girls, and sometimes Miss May would have the winners of the previous matches choose teams. Two Fridays in a row, Caroline found herself standing next to Charlie Ingalls, competing for first place. The first Friday Caroline spelled him down after only two words. But the next Friday Charlie seemed determined to stay standing. He spelled each word Miss May gave him with great care.

"Consequence," Miss May said.

"Consequence," Charlie repeated, and then he spelled the word. "C-O-N-S-E-Q-U-E-N-C-E."

Then it was Caroline's turn.

"Continent," Miss May said, and slowly Caroline said the letters.

The afternoon wore on, and each time Charlie spelled a word, a muffled cheer was heard from the boys' side of the room. Each time Caroline spelled a word correctly, a quiet ripple went through the girls' side.

At last Miss May gave Charlie the word "corroborate."

"Corroborate," Charlie said slowly. He ran his hands through his hair, standing it on end. "C-O-R-O-B-O-R-A-T-E," he spelled.

"That is not correct,' Miss May said, and a few gasps were heard. Miss May turned to Caroline. "The word is 'corroborate.'"

Caroline took a deep breath. "Corroborate," she said, and then evenly she said each letter. "C-O-R-R-O-B-O-R-A-T-E."

Miss May nodded. "We have a winner," she said.

The whole room erupted.

"Aw, Charlie, you let a girl beat you," Jamie called.

"I'll get you next time, Caroline Quiner," Charlie said on his way back to his seat. But he did not say it in a mean way. He gave Caroline his friendly grin, and his sharp blue eyes held a twinkle.

Now that winter had really arrived, the girls, big and small, stayed inside with Miss May during noon recess while the boys went outside to play. They sat in a tight circle around the stove, chatting or working on some knitting or embroidery they had brought. Sometimes Miss May sat quietly apart reading a book or writing in her day journal with her pearl-handled pen, and sometimes she sat with them and talked about her home. She said that she was used to cold weather.

"Albany can be quite frigid in the winter months," she explained. "But it is the time to go visiting. Everyone goes from house to house, surprising their hosts with a visiting party. The streets are alive with the sound of tinkling bells as the sleighs and cutters go whizzing by."

Caroline thought about this, and she could tell the other girls were thinking about it too. How jolly it sounded! To live in a bustling town and to have so many friends to surprise with a visit. For two Christmases in a row the Kelloggs had invited them for tea and cookies. They had never made a surprise visit, though.

In any case, it looked as though visiting would have to wait. That very night a heavy snow began to fall, and it did not let up for several days. Each morning Pa and the boys had to shovel their way out of the house and make a new path to the barn. In some parts of the clearing the drifts were almost up to Caroline's waist.

It took longer and longer to reach the schoolhouse in the morning, until one day they could no longer walk through the deep drifts. Pa quickly made a rough sleigh, and Joseph drove them to school and back. But even the oxen had a hard time plodding through the snow.

Caroline was surprised when Mr. Kellogg appeared at the schoolhouse door one day at noon. He took off his hat and shook the snow from his long overcoat, smiling at Margaret and the other girls sitting around the stove.

Then he took a deep breath and looked about the room before settling his eyes on Miss May.

"I know how much our youngsters enjoy

having you teach them, but it's getting too cold, and the snow is too deep to keep school open. I am afraid I must close the school down for a time. We do not want our children to freeze to death, either on the road to the schoolhouse or inside its very walls."

Caroline looked back and forth from Mr. Kellogg to Miss May. Her heart seemed to sink inside her chest. She could not believe school would really be closed.

"I understand completely," Miss May said, but Caroline could tell she was disappointed.

"Good." Mr. Kellogg smiled. "I promise you that we will resume school as soon as we possibly can."

When the boys returned from noon recess, Miss May made the announcement. "I am truly sorry, but I am afraid we cannot compete against Mother Nature."

When school was dismissed that day, the boys gave a loud shout. Even though they liked Miss May, it was something to be told not to come to school indefinitely. Now they would have all day to go sledding and ice-skating and have snowball fights.

"Well, I suppose Mr. Kellogg knows best," Mother said after they had reached home and told her the news. "But a closed school does not mean a closed mind. I expect you all to continue to study your lessons in the mornings."

Thomas looked as if he were about to complain, but he quickly thought better of it. Mother was wearing her serious look, the one she always wore when she talked of how important it was to have an education. That evening she spoke with Miss May, and it was decided that in the mornings they would have their very own school right there in the kitchen.

"Then you are free to do as you like in the afternoons, as long as Pa does not need you," Mother said.

Caroline felt glad, and she could tell Martha and Eliza were happy too.

That very night another snowstorm hit. Day after day the wind howled and the snow fell. No one left the little house except for Pa and Joseph and Henry. Caroline was worried about her chickens, but Pa said they were getting along fine inside their snug henhouse.

At first it was good to have lessons to distract them. Miss May gave them riddles and word puzzles along with their regular lessons. At night she read to them from the books or literary magazines she had brought. There was one poem that frightened Caroline, but the boys loved it. It was "The Raven" by Edgar Allan Poe, and it made the hair on the back of Caroline's neck stand on end. Especially when Miss May's voice ominously spoke the words, "'Quoth the Raven, "Nevermore."'"

But despite the lessons and readings, after a week of staying inside, they became listless. Even Caroline had trouble focusing on her reader. The letters seemed to swim before her, and she often had to ask Miss May to repeat a question.

"What we need is a little party," Mother said one afternoon, when she saw the children sitting around the warm stove, staring off at nothing in particular.

"A party?" Eliza asked.

They watched as Mother went into the pantry and came back carrying flour and eggs and a mixing bowl.

"It is someone's birthday, after all!" Mother exclaimed, looking at Caroline.

Caroline nearly fell out of her chair. With the snow and the long, dozy days, she had forgotten about her birthday!

Now she and Martha and Eliza and Miss May began to help Mother. First they made a beautiful white-sugar cake. Then they made a fine venison stew from some of the meat that had been smoked for the winter. Caroline made the biscuits, and Mother said they could have some watermelon pickles.

After supper Mother brought out a flat rectangular package wrapped in plain brown paper and tied with a string.

"This is from your Pa and me," Mother said.

"What is it?" Caroline gasped.

"Open it and see!" Thomas shouted, and everyone laughed.

Caroline was careful not to tear the wrapping paper so that it could be used to make more notebook pages. Inside was the beautiful day journal she had admired at the fair. Caroline could not speak. She ran her hands over the marbled cover.

"A little bird told me this might be a nice gift for a young lady," Mother said.

"Oh, thank you," Caroline whispered. Then she looked up from Pa's and Mother's smiling faces to Miss May. "Oh, thank you," she said again. Martha and Eliza crowded around to look at the gift.

"I wish I could play a fiddle like that Charlie Ingalls," Henry said. "Then this would really be a party."

"Well, your mother sings like a bird," Pa said. "I reckon she could lead us in a song or two, and that would keep us lively."

Caroline felt such happiness inside as Mother began to sing "Bonny Doon," one of Caroline's favorites, and they all joined in, even Pa. As she sang, Caroline thought about how much things had changed for them over the past few years. When Pa had first married Mother, he was always solemn. Now his face was smiling and his voice was raised in song.

They sang well into the evening and ended with "For she's a jolly good fellow," in honor of Caroline's birthday. Mother said Caroline might write in her journal before going to bed. So she sat at the kitchen table, took out her quill and sharpened the point, then dipped the tip into the ink bottle.

Slowly she wrote her name along the top of the inside cover. The quill did not make as fine a line as Caroline would have liked. She thought of Miss May's pearl-handled pen and suddenly wished she had been given a real pen to go with the day journal. Immediately she felt ashamed. She had been given such a beautiful gift. How could she wish for more?

She dipped her quill again, and on the first page she wrote:

December 12, 1851
Today I was given this little book in honor of my twelfth birthday.

That was all she could think to write.

Suddenly she wondered if she would ever fill up a whole book. But she supposed she had all the time in the world. Carefully she blotted the ink and blew on it until it was dry. Then she closed the book and took it with her upstairs. She tucked it neatly inside the drawer where she kept her extra petticoats and apron and stockings.

Winter School

In the morning the snow had stopped, and the sun came out to shine on the white world.

Caroline went to stand beside Miss May as she gazed out the frosted kitchen window.

"Why, it's like something out of a fairy tale," Miss May said, and Caroline had to agree.

The snow- and ice-covered trees looked like giant white feathers bending over the clearing, and the ground itself was like a thick, sparkling carpet. Caroline had seen snowy woods before, of course, but somehow with

Miss May there as witness, the scene seemed especially dazzling.

Pa and Joseph and Henry were not so dazzled, however. It took most of the morning to break new paths to do the chores. Caroline went out to see to her chickens. It felt good to go outside at last. The air made her lungs ache, and right away her nose and the tips of her fingers began to tingle with cold, but she felt awake for the first time in days.

When she was on her way back to the house, she caught sight of two figures tramping through the drifts, pulling a sled behind them with a third figure perched on top. They were all wearing snowshoes and were completely bundled from head to toe, so Caroline could not tell who they were. But when they called out a hearty "Hellooooo," she recognized them right away. It was Peter, Charlie, and Jamie Ingalls.

Inside the lean-to they unwound their many layers and took off their snowshoes.

"We came to see how you folks are making

out," Peter said. He had brought a mincemeat pie from his ma.

"That's what Peter came for. Jamie and I came to see if you wanted to go sledding," Charlie said.

"We're still in school," Thomas announced importantly. He was sitting in his place at the table with his reader, waiting for lessons to begin.

"School?" Jamie gasped.

"School's out—haven't you heard?" Charlie said.

"Not for us," Thomas explained, and Caroline noticed that he sounded a little proud of the fact.

Peter surveyed the table with all the readers and spellers open upon it. "I guess that's what you get for boarding the teacher. Schooling when school is out." But he said it in a quiet, joking way, and they all laughed, even Miss May.

"I suppose we can dismiss class today, since we have the first visitors we've seen in a while," Miss May said.

Mother agreed to let them go out and play after she had given the Ingalls boys some hot tea to warm their bones.

So Caroline bundled up once more and helped Eliza wind the muffler around her face to keep out the cold. At first Martha said she would stay and help Mother in the kitchen, but then at the last minute she decided to go outside too. Caroline thought it must be hard to be a grown-up in winter, when the snow was so inviting.

Joseph and Henry brought out their sleds and led the way to the little hill that lay beyond the last field. It took a while to make a path through the thick snow so that the sleds could glide down the hill without getting stuck. But soon they were whooshing so fast, it felt to Caroline as if she were flying.

Peter and Charlie and Jamie stayed to dinner, and then they started for home, promising to come back the next afternoon and bring their sisters with them.

"It's easy getting across the river, now that it's froze up, and as long as it doesn't snow again, we've made a path to your door," Charlie said.

So the next day, after lessons and after dinner, Eliza and Thomas stood watching for the Ingallses at the window. As soon as they caught sight of the bundled figures, they shouted, and everyone began to put on their warm things.

Charlie and Peter each had brought a sled this time, and they were pulling Jamie and two of the girls. Caroline could hardly tell which sister was which, since only their eyes peered out of the mufflers.

"It's so good to see you!" the Ingalls girls exclaimed as soon as they reached the clearing.

"Ma wouldn't let Docia come," Polly said.

"And golly, did she put up a fuss!" Lydia added.

"Let's go!" Thomas yelled.

Nearly the whole afternoon was spent rushing down the hill and trudging up it again. Sometimes the the sled would hit a log, and then Caroline and the others would go tumbling out into the snow. After a while Martha and Lydia went back inside, but Caroline and Polly and Eliza made snow angels in the clearing.

"Hurry and sit by the stove!" Mother said when at last it grew too cold to stay outside a moment more.

Mother gave them hot tea with warm milk and honey and little heart-shaped cakes she had made. Afterward, the boys sat taking turns at the checkerboard while Caroline and Eliza and showed Polly around the house.

"I wish we had a parlor," Polly said, sighing.

"We didn't have one when we first came here," Caroline said. "We lived in a tiny little cabin."

For the rest of the afternoon Caroline and Martha and Eliza stayed upstairs in their bedroom, showing Lydia and Polly their dolls and the newspapers and the *Godey's* they had collected. When it was time to go, Lydia and Polly asked Mother if Caroline and Martha and Eliza and the boys might all come to their house the next day.

"Does your mother know about this invitation?" Mother asked.

"Oh, yes," Lydia replied. "She said it would

be good to see some new faces."

And so the next day, after dinner, Caroline and Eliza and Martha piled onto the sled, and Joseph and Henry and Thomas took turns pulling them through the woods. Ice covered the bare branches of the trees, shimmering in the sunlight. They did not see any animals about, but there were rabbit and deer tracks zigzagging through the snow. When they reached the river, they saw that it was frozen over, with rocks and logs sticking up through the ice.

Once across, they followed the path the Ingallses had made through the deep drifts, and almost right away they came into a small clearing. In the middle of the clearing, surrounded by a split-rail fence, sat a large two-story cabin. It was much bigger than the cabin Caroline had lived in when she and her family had first come to the woods. It was solidly built of fat yellow logs. It had a slanting roof, a lean-to over the door, and two small glass windows. There was a rock chimney built up one side of the cabin, and smoke billowed forth,

filling the woods with a good hickory scent.
Beyond the cabin was a log barn.

Caroline saw a face blur at one window, and
then the little lean-to door opened.

"Come in and warm yourselves by the fire,"
Mrs. Ingalls called in her cheery voice.

Once they had taken off their outer garments, Martha gave Mrs. Ingalls the applesauce cake Mother had sent.

"Oh, how lovely!" Mrs. Ingalls said.

Caroline looked around curiously. They had
stepped into a large square kitchen with neatly
chinked walls and gleaming new plank floors.
A handsome stone fireplace took up nearly one
whole wall, and a black iron cookstove sat in
one corner. There was a dish dresser with tin
and pewter dishes stacked neatly on the
shelves. Braids of onions and peppers hung
from the rafters. There was a large pinewood
table in the center of the room, with a bright
calico cloth covering it. Two rocking chairs and
a cradle sat near the hearth. Baby George was
sleeping in the cradle.

Lydia and Polly showed the girls the rest of

the house. There was a cozy bedroom right off the kitchen where Mr. and Mrs. Ingalls slept. And there was a pantry with shelves and drawers very much like the one Pa had made for Mother.

Upstairs was one long room. Two quilts had been strung up in the middle of the room to make two separate bedrooms, one for the girls and one for the boys. On the girls' side there was a chest of drawers and one large bed, with the quilt Lydia and Polly had brought to the fair covering it.

"This is my doll," Docia said, showing them a rag doll with curly black yarn hair, black button eyes, and a smiling red mouth. She wore a red gingham dress. "Her name is Rebecca."

Back in the kitchen Mrs. Ingalls sat them all at the big table and served hot apple cider and little cookies that melted in Caroline's mouth. Caroline thought it did not matter that there was no parlor, the kitchen felt so friendly and spacious.

Then they bundled up again and went out into the bright cold. Mrs. Ingalls agreed to let

Docia and little Hiram go out for a while. They played game after game of fox and geese until they were all breathless and panting in the frosty air.

"We'd better head home," Joseph said at last. "It's nearly time for chores."

"Let's meet at the river tomorrow," Charlie suggested. "We've got ice skates we could share if you don't have any."

"We've got our own!" Thomas proudly said. "Santa Claus brought them to us!"

So the next day after chores and morning lessons and dinner, they took their skates and went back to the river. The Ingallses were already there. Caroline and her brothers and sisters were dressed in so many layers, they had to help each other buckle their ice skates on over their boots.

"At least we'll be padded if we fall!" Martha joked.

Peter and Charlie showed them a game called knocking at the cobbler's door. It was played by trying to slide in a straight line along the ice on one foot while stamping on the ice again and again with the other foot.

It was not easy to skate on one foot over the rough surface of the river. The girls decided to sit on a log and watch as the boys finished their game. Peter showed them another game called wounded soldier. They had to kneel on one knee and see how far they could slide.

"The millpond is much nicer to skate on," Martha told Lydia and Polly.

"Our pa helped build the mill," Eliza added. "Have you been there yet?"

"Oh, yes," Lydia said. "We went with Pa when he bought some wheat."

"Maybe it was our wheat you were buying," Caroline said.

"Maybe so," Polly replied.

The girls promised to go skating there once they could get through the snow to Concord again.

"I miss going to school, and I miss Miss May," Polly said. "And it's no fun studying on our own. I wish we could join you in the mornings. Ma does, too. She says she's tired of having us all underfoot."

"Maybe you can," Caroline said. That night

she told Mother what Polly had said, and Mother spoke to Miss May.

"I would be happy to expand our little winter school," Miss May said.

First thing in the morning Henry left to tell the Ingallses. Soon after breakfast Charlie and Lydia and Polly and Jamie and Docia arrived with their books. Only Peter was missing.

"Since he turned eighteen, he told Pa he doesn't need any more learning," Charlie explained.

It was crowded around the kitchen table, but Caroline liked having their very own little winter school, as Miss May had called it. After lessons they ate dinner together. The Ingallses had brought theirs in dinner pails. Then they went out to play in the snow.

On Friday Miss May announced they would have a spelldown, just like they'd had at the real schoolhouse.

Caroline took a deep breath and glanced down the length of the table to where Charlie was sitting. Charlie was looking right at her. He had one eyebrow raised, and he was grinning. Caroline glanced quickly down at her books. Then she felt a poke in her side. Martha gave her an encouraging smile and a nod. Caroline smiled back. She knew she would beat Charlie just as she had done before.

Miss May invited Mother and Pa to come in and watch the spelldown. Mother sat in her rocker near the stove and took up her knitting. Pa settled down into a chair beside her and rubbed his hands together.

"I haven't had a chance to see a good spell-down in a while," he said.

Miss May had the small group of scholars line up along the wall in front of the hearth. "Now we shall begin," she said, taking up her speller, and glancing through it till she found a starting place.

As always, the first words were easy. No one sat down for several rounds, but then Thomas missed a word. Jamie sat down next, followed by Henry and Eliza.

Caroline kept glancing at Mother. She noticed that Mother's knitting needles paused each time one of the children faltered over a letter. When Caroline was silent for just a moment, wondering if there were two t's or one in "buttress," she noticed wrinkles forming across Mother's brow. The wrinkles smoothed out as soon as Caroline had finished spelling the word correctly.

Soon Caroline found herself standing alone in front of the hearth beside Charlie. He gave her a quick sideways glance, but Caroline kept her eyes on Miss May. She was determined to stay standing, especially here in her own home.

"Cautious," Miss May said, and Caroline spelled the word correctly.

"Cavalcade" went to Charlie and he remained standing.

Just as in the schoolhouse, the girls were rooting for Caroline and the boys were rooting for Charlie. Eliza let out a little squeal each time Caroline finished a word, and Thomas and Jamie banged their fists on the table each time Miss May told Charlie that his spelling was correct.

The morning grew late. Caroline did not look at Charlie as the words went back and forth between them, but finally, as Miss May paused to turn the pages of her book, Caroline turned her head a little and caught Charlie's eye. He gave her a wink and ran a hand through his thick dark hair, standing it on end.

Quickly Caroline looked away. She didn't understand why Charlie made her feel like giggling when she was determined to spell him down.

"Incessant," Miss May said, bringing her head up and fixing her serious gaze on Caroline. "The word is 'incessant.'"

Caroline was so sure Charlie could not beat her, she rushed through the letters without thinking.

"I-N-C-E-S-A-N-T," she spelled.

In the deep silence that followed, Caroline realized Mother's knitting needles had stopped and she saw the wrinkles form on

Mother's brow. Instantly she knew she had made a mistake. She had left out an "s"!

"That is incorrect," Miss May said, and Caroline felt as if she had suddenly been plunged under water. Sounds became muffled. She could hear the boys cheering and the girls letting out little gasps of disbelief. But the sounds were very far away. Caroline felt herself blinking her eyes open and closed; then it was as if she had been thrust up to the surface again. She gasped a little, and Miss May's voice was very loud.

"Charlie, the word is 'incessant.'"

"I-N-C-E-S-S-A-N-T," Charlie spelled slowly and clearly.

"That is correct," Miss May said. "We have a new winner."

The boys rushed forward to congratulate Charlie. Caroline felt Eliza tugging on her arm.

"I don't believe he beat you!" Eliza said.

"Shush!" Martha said to Eliza. Then she took Caroline's hand and patted it gently. "Don't worry," she whispered. "It's okay to lose now and then."

Miss May announced that lessons were over for the day, and she thanked Mother and Pa for attending their spelldown. Caroline glanced at Mother as she stood to congratulate Charlie. Never in her life had Caroline felt so ashamed. To think she had been spelled down here in her own kitchen! She wanted to rush up to Mother and tell her that she had never ever lost before, but she knew that boasting was wrong.

The boys began to put on their coats and mufflers and hats to go outside, and the girls followed them. Slowly Caroline began to bundle herself up. She did not feel like playing, but she could not stay inside, or everyone would know she was a sore loser.

Outside in the clearing, Caroline wanted to avoid Charlie. But he came right up to her. "I did it!" he said, laughing. "I finally spelled down Caroline Quiner!"

Caroline felt tears stinging her eyes. She looked away and was about to rush past, but then she saw that Charlie was only teasing her. His blue eyes were not mean but friendly.

Spelldowns were a friendly competition, after all. And it did not hurt to lose now and then, as Martha said.

Caroline smiled and then raised her chin in the air. "You won't do it again, Charles *the Second*!" she teased back.

Charlie let out a loud guffaw, then turned and rushed ahead to catch up to Henry.

Attending their little winter school and playing with the Ingallses every afternoon made the days go very quickly. It was difficult to keep track of time, even though Caroline tried to write in her day journal as often as she could. She at least made sure that she noted the important dates. When Christmas came, Caroline took a quiet moment to herself during the merry bustle.

December 25, 1851
   Each Christmas is better than the last, I believe. When I said so to Mother, she told me it is because I am growing up.

And when New Year's Day arrived, it was

hard for Caroline to believe a whole new year was beginning.

January 1, 1852
As I write, my pen falters over the date.
1852! I wonder what this new year will
bring. I pray that it will be a year of plenty,
as Pa predicted.

One night, as Caroline was closing her day journal, Mother came into the kitchen to tell her it was time for bed.

"You are enjoying your time with Miss May, are you not?" Mother asked.

"Oh, yes!" Caroline exclaimed. "It's like having our very own governess, just like in *Jane Eyre*, the book Miss May read to us."

Mother gave a little smile and looked over Caroline's head, as if she were remembering something. "And just like your grandma Tucker had when she was a little girl in Scotland," she said.

"Grandma Tucker had a governess?" Caroline asked.

"Yes, she did," Mother answered, nodding and laughing a little. "She liked one of her governesses, as I recall. But she would have preferred to go to school with her brothers, if her father had allowed it."

School was so very important to Mother, Caroline could hardly imagine *not* being allowed to go. "Oh, Mother, I want to be a schoolteacher when I am old enough," she suddenly said. "Just like Miss May."

Mother's eyes were smiling, and she reached out to gently smooth back a wisp of Caroline's hair. "Miss May tells me you are an excellent scholar, Caroline," she said. "I have no doubt you would make a wonderful teacher, if that is what you truly want to do. But studying to be a teacher means that you must put your lessons first. Do you understand?"

"Yes," Caroline said solemnly. Suddenly she felt that it was her duty to be the best scholar she could be. For the rest of that week she did not go out to play with the others, but stayed inside and studied her reader. Henry teased her and so did Charlie, but she did not care.

She made a promise to herself to be diligent and serious.

But then the surprise visiting began, and it was nearly impossible to stick to her resolution. One could not study every single moment of the day, after all. Especially when the air rang with the jolly sound of sleigh bells coming through the wintry woods.

Surprise Visiting

First it was the Wighams, gliding over the drifts in a handsome new cutter. And then it was the Atwoods and the Nielsens. They all stopped and visited awhile, bringing news of Concord. Folks were beginning to venture out to rustle up some company, even if the snow was still thick and the days were bitterly cold.

"It's just like back home," Miss May said.

"The girls must have told their folks about your surprise visiting back east," Caroline said.

"I suppose you're right," Miss May agreed.

One day the Spiveys came. Caroline was just as glad to see Nell as Martha was, but she could not feel happy about seeing Mrs. Spivey. Her face burned as she watched Mrs. Spivey look Miss May up and down when they were introduced.

The boys went out to play while Pa and Mr. Spivey stayed in the kitchen to smoke their pipes. Caroline and Martha helped carry the tea and the little cakes Mother had made into the parlor. As soon as the food had been served on Mother's good pewter dishes, Mrs. Spivey turned to Miss May.

"I have heard that you allow the children play games in school." Her mouth was turned down and her voice was harsh. It was as if she had just taken a bite of something unpleasant.

Caroline quickly glanced at Miss May to see how she would react to such a sudden attack. But Miss May had not lost her composure. She smiled and nodded. "That is correct," she said brightly. "I believe that word games, properly used, can help stimulate learning."

"When I was a girl, our schoolmaster stimulated learning through discipline." Mrs. Spivey sniffed.

"Discipline is important," Miss May replied, and her tone did not lose its cheerfulness. "But I do not believe one needs to resort to the switch to instill it in the classroom. I do not believe in frightening scholars into learning."

"Sometimes the switch is the only way to get youngsters to mind," Mrs. Spivey said.

Caroline felt her stomach twisting into knots. She wanted to shout at the horrible Mrs. Spivey. She did not see how Miss May could remain so composed.

Miss May took a sip of tea before replying in a careful voice. "There is a growing concern among teachers in the east that physical punishment is not the proper way to encourage our young people to learn. We must bring them to love learning, rather than beat them to it."

"'Spare the rod, spoil the child,' I always say," Mrs. Spivey replied.

"Many teachers back east are now devotees of the educator Lyman Cobb, who has written a book called *The Evil Tendencies of Corporal Punishment as a Means of Moral Discipline in Families and Schools*. The author lists some sixty sound arguments against the practice of beating children. I could lend you the book if you like."

Mrs. Spivey clucked her tongue and shook her head. "I've no time for such reading," she said coldly. "I will give you this, however. You have been lucky not to have any bullies among the big boys here in Concord. In many schools the teacher is run off when he cannot maintain order."

Suddenly Caroline could no longer remain silent. "Miss May has no trouble maintaining order," she said hotly. "We love her, and we have learned a great deal."

"Caroline!" Mother admonished in a stern voice.

Caroline looked down at her hands. She felt ashamed of herself. She knew it was wrong to interrupt grown-ups when they were speaking. But surely it was also wrong for Mrs. Spivey to be so rude to Miss May! There was a moment of silence, and then Mother smoothly steered the conversation to the weather. When Caroline looked up again, Miss May gave her a small, secret smile that made her feel better.

That night, long after the visitors had left, the girls were upstairs brushing out their hair. Mother came into their room and sat on their bed. She patted the place beside her for Caroline to sit.

"I know you only wanted to defend Miss May," she said. "But you must remember your manners always, in every situation."

"Yes, ma'am," Caroline mumbled. She glanced at Mother's face and decided to say more. "It seems to me that Mrs. Spivey did not remember her manners."

"That may well be," Mother said. "But that does not change how you must behave."

"Yes, ma'am," Caroline whispered, though it did not seem fair.

Eliza scooted in between Mother and Caroline. "But why is Mrs. Spivey so . . . mean?" she asked in a small voice.

Mother sighed. "Some people will always

choose to look at things from a narrow per-
spective. They do not like change or new
ideas. You will meet these people throughout
your life. But it does no good to argue with
them. Happy is as happy does. You must think
of how to meet opposition with cheerfulness."

When Mother had finished speaking, they
were quiet for a while, and then Eliza said,
"We have not done any visiting ourselves."

Mother cocked her head to one side and
gave a mischievous smile. "Let us see what
tomorrow brings." But she would say no more,
except good night.

The next morning the girls waited for a sign
that they were going visiting. At last, after the
dinner dishes had been wiped and put away,
it came. Mother packed the dried-cherry pie she
had made that morning into a basket, and Pa
brought the wagon sled around to the front door.

"Where are we going? Where are we going?"
the girls asked as they piled into the back
along with Miss May and the boys, wrapping
the quilts and buffalo robes about themselves.

"You shall see soon enough," Mother replied mysteriously from the wagon seat.

Pa sent Slow and Ready plodding along the path to the river, and Caroline knew where they were headed. To the Ingallses!

It was a quick drive since the children had beaten out a path over the past weeks. When they arrived at the clearing, the door to the cabin opened and Mr. Ingalls stepped outside and called, "Welcome, friends! The wife was just thinking it was time to pay you folks a visit, and here you are!"

No sooner had they removed their wraps and entered the handsome kitchen, with its great stone fireplace and lovely spicy smell, than the *tinkle tinkle* of sleigh bells was heard outside.

"My goodness!" Mrs. Ingalls exclaimed. "I am glad I had the foresight to do extra baking this morning!"

It was the Wighams in their fine cutter. There were happy greetings and hearty laughter all around as the Wighams came inside. And no sooner had *they* taken off *their* wraps than more bells were heard. It was the Taylors, whom Caroline had seen at church on Sundays but never spoken to. They were a young couple, like the Wighams. And just like the Wighams, they had a baby boy.

"They are our closest neighbors on this side of the river," Polly whispered to Caroline. "They're Yorkers, like us."

Mrs. Taylor was small and plump with yellow spaniel curls framing a pleasant round face. She wore a handsome green calico dress. Her husband was short as well, with sandy hair and a neatly trimmed beard. Their baby, Moses, had a chubby, smiling face and fat little hands that reached for everything close by.

"We're nearly full to bursting!" Mrs. Ingalls said, her brown eyes laughing. "Now we shall have a party!"

Lydia and Polly helped their mother serve up hot spiced apple cider and bowls of warm popped corn that had been buttered and salted. Then they ate some of Mother's dried-cherry pie and Mrs. Wigham's apple turnovers and Mrs. Taylor's dainty cookies and Mrs. Ingalls' vinegar pie. After that the ladies settled down in front of the fire with their knitting and sewing while the men stood near the stove talking of the spring planting to come. The boys put on their wraps to go sledding, but the girls decided to stay inside. Martha and Lydia stayed downstairs with the ladies, but Caroline and Polly and Eliza took Docia and Hiram and the three babies upstairs to play. They sat the babies on a quilt on the floor.

"Let's play school," Polly said. "I think Caroline should be the teacher."

"Well, all right," Caroline agreed, smiling a little.

Polly brought out her books and slates while Caroline arranged George and Daniel and Moses together in the first row of school.

"You are my first primer class," Caroline said, and the babies smiled and cooed back at her.

Docia and Eliza sat in the next row, and Polly sat behind them. Caroline took Polly's schoolbooks and gave Docia a poem to memorize. She had Polly and Eliza draw pictures on their slates, and then she sat down and tried to teach the babies their ABC's, but they were more interested in trying to tear the pages from the book.

"I guess being a teacher is harder than I thought," Caroline said, laughing.

"I'm tired of school!" Docia said crossly.

So Docia got Rebecca and two other dolls that had been Polly and Lydia's. Polly brought out a box of little wooden animals that her pa had whittled and let the babies play with them. There were bears and bobcats and wolves, and there were horses and cows and pigs. The wood was smooth and shiny in places from many hands playing with them over the years.

When the babies began to fuss, the girls took them back to their mothers. Caroline noticed it was growing dark outside the window, and she thought they would be heading home soon, but it seemed that no one wanted to leave the cozy kitchen.

"Might as well make a night of it," Mr. Ingalls said, and Mrs. Ingalls gaily added, "We'll rustle up a quick supper and then—who knows?—maybe we'll have a little dancing."

"Dancing!" Mrs. Taylor exclaimed, and she

giggled like a girl. "Why, I haven't been dancing since we left New York."

"My son Charlie makes some fine dancing music on his fiddle," Mr. Ingalls said, and Caroline noticed how proud he sounded.

"Well, then, ladies, let's get to work!" Mrs. Ingalls said. "But first we need a little room in here!" She put her hands on her hips, and her brown eyes flashed merrily as she looked her husband up and down.

"Guess we know when we're not wanted!" Pa joked.

Mr. Ingalls shook his head and chuckled. "Reckon we're not too old to do some sledding with the boys." They put on their coats and headed out into the cold.

Now the ladies began to bustle around the stove. When Martha asked what she could do to help, Mrs. Ingalls said, "Too many skirts in the kitchen as it is! Why don't you girls take the babies upstairs till we call for you."

Caroline could tell Martha felt that she should be allowed to stay in the kitchen with the ladies, but Martha did not say a word.

Instead, she and Lydia led the way upstairs, carrying the babies. Caroline and Polly and Eliza settled on the floor again, playing with the little wooden figures. They talked of the visitors who had come calling over the past week. After a time the smell of good things cooking wafted up from below. Caroline's stomach was grumbling.

At last they heard Mother calling to them and a dinner bell being rung outside. The men and boys tramped back in, and the girls came down the stairs. The kitchen was warm and smelled wonderful. The kitchen table was laden with plates and bowls and platters of food.

"Some of us will have to eat standing up, I'm afraid!" Mrs. Ingalls said.

But that did not matter. The surprise supper was delicious, and there was plenty to go around. After every last morsel was eaten and the plates were put away, Mr. Ingalls turned to Charlie and said, "I told these folks you might be persuaded to bring out your fiddle, son, and play a few dance tunes."

Charlie's whole face lit up. "I'd be happy to,

Pa!" He rushed upstairs to get his fiddle box while the rest hurried to move the table and the chairs from the center of the room.

Caroline watched as Charlie tenderly rosined the bow and then plucked a few notes, listening and tightening up the strings. At last he grinned and nodded his head, satisfied that the fiddle was in tune.

"Here we go!" he called out, bowing a little and jerking the bow in the air.

The notes started up quick and lively. Everyone in the room began to clap along. Caroline did not recognize the tune, but she could hardly keep her feet still, just the same.

Neither could anyone else. Mr. Ingalls led his wife out onto the dance floor, and then the Wighams and the Taylors joined in. There was a colorful swirl of skirts and a *tap-tap-tap*ping of heels and a *clomp-clomp*ing of boots.

Henry turned to Caroline and bowed and said, "May I have this dance, miss?"

Caroline giggled as she and her brother jigged the steps Mother had taught them long ago in Brookfield.

When that song ended, Charlie struck up another right away. It was "Turkey in the Straw." This time Henry danced with Polly and Caroline stood near the wall, clapping and singing the words to the song out loud with the others.

> *"Went out to milk, and I didn't know how.*
> *I milked the goat instead of the cow.*
> *A monkey sittin' on a pile of straw*
> *A-winkin' at his mother-in-law.*
> *Turkey in the straw, turkey in the hay,*
> *Roll 'em up and twist 'em up a high*
>   *tuckahaw,*
> *And twist 'em up a tune called 'Turkey in*
>   *the Straw.'"*

Now there were more bodies on the dance floor. Peter had jumped up and was dancing with Martha. And Joseph was dancing with Lydia. Mr. Ingalls had asked Miss May to dance, and she cut a very graceful figure as her slender waist stayed straight above her twirling gray skirt.

But Caroline could hardly believe her eyes when she saw Pa dancing with Mother. Pa could not move as quickly as the other dancers. His leg dragged behind, and his body was stiff, but he looked happy, and so did Mother. Her face was flushed a lovely pink, and her green eyes sparkled in the firelight as her skirts whirled around her.

> *"Came to a river and I couldn't get across,*
> *Paid five dollars for a blind old hoss;*
> *Wouldn't go ahead nor he wouldn't stand*
> *still,*
> *So he went up and down like an old saw*
> *mill.*
> *Turkey in the straw, turkey in the hay,*
> *Roll 'em up and twist 'em up a high*
> *tuckahaw,*
> *And twist 'em up a tune called 'Turkey in*
> *the Straw.'"*

Each time the fiddle stopped, the dancers shouted for more, and then Charlie would grin and pause to wipe his forehead. Then the bow would jerk into the air and another jaunty melody would make the room clap and cheer.

"That boy's a mighty good fiddler," Caroline heard Mr. Taylor say. She thought of the first time she had heard Charlie practicing his fiddle in the woods by himself. She supposed that the practicing, even on a Sunday, was worth it, because Charlie seemed to know exactly what songs to play to please the crowd, and the notes spilled out seamlessly from the honey-colored fiddle.

It grew so late, the babies and the younger children fell asleep. Caroline wondered if they would end up spending the night at the Ingallses', but then Pa said he would go out and get the wagon ready, and the other men followed suit.

"Thank you for a lovely party!" Mrs. Taylor said.

"Oh, yes," Mrs. Wigham added. "I don't remember when I've had such fun."

They all agreed that surprise parties were the best kind.

Spring Rush

All of a sudden, it seemed, spring was in the air. The sun began to warm the earth, and the snow began to melt.

One afternoon Mr. Kellogg came to tell them that the schoolhouse would be opening the following Monday.

"The school board is anxious for you to begin the next term," Mr. Kellogg told Miss May. "Particularly since your first was cut short."

"I have enjoyed teaching my small class here," Miss May said, "but I am very happy that the schoolhouse will be open again. I suppose I will need to pack my things, then?" She looked questioningly at Mr. Kellogg.

Suddenly Caroline felt a great sadness wash over her. She had known all along that Miss May would be going to stay with the Atwoods, but somehow she had thought of her departure as far off in the future. Now the future was here, and it did not seem right. Miss May was nearly like family now. Caroline could not imagine her going off to board somewhere else.

"Well, that is also what I have come to speak to you about," Mr. Kellogg said. "The Atwoods have decided to leave Concord and go farther west. And so I will need to find another family to board you for the next term. I would offer our own home, but I am afraid that Mrs. Kellogg is still not well enough after the birth of our Sally."

Caroline was very sorry to hear about Mrs. Kellogg. Mother said that she would go to see her that very week.

"May I go too?" Eliza asked. Caroline knew she had missed seeing Margaret.

"I am sure they would be glad of the company," Mr. Kellogg said, smiling. "They were both sorry to miss out on the surprise visiting we heard so much about."

"It seems to me that Miss May is already settled in here," Pa suddenly spoke up. "It would be no trouble for us to continue to board her over the next term."

Caroline caught her breath and looked back and forth from Pa to Mr. Kellogg to Miss May.

"Why, I would not want to be a burden," Miss May said.

"You are not a burden," Pa replied. "Seems to me you've given these children a good deal of learning they might not have gotten over the past few months."

And it was settled. Miss May would not be leaving them! Caroline was so happy, she could hardly sit still for the rest of Mr. Kellogg's visit. After he had left, Caroline rushed up to Miss May and gave her a hug.

"Goodness!" Miss May said, but she returned Caroline's warm embrace.

"I am so glad you're not leaving," Caroline exclaimed.

"We all are," Mother added.

Now the days continued as they had in the fall. Each morning they walked to school with Miss May, and then returned with her in the afternoon. The great patches of snow began to shrink until there were only small bits of white. Everywhere a constant *tap-tap-tap*ping could be heard as snow and ice melted from trees and roofs. The ground thawed and soon became thick with mud. The river swelled, rushing and gurgling and overflowing its bank. There was flooding in the low parts of the field.

"We'll have to wait awhile to do our plowing," Pa said. "The sun needs to dry up the ground some."

Soon the older boys stopped coming to school. Even though planting would be late that year, there was much to do to prepare. Joseph and Henry went about the fields with their hoes and pickaxes, grubbing the stumps.

They mended the split-rail fences that had been pushed down by the snow, and they went with Pa to the Watertown market to buy two new pigs and more geese.

Caroline missed the older boys after they were gone from school. The games were more lively when the schoolhouse was full, and Charlie Ingalls made her work harder to make first place in the spelldowns.

As spring took hold, there seemed to be a rush. Every day on the way to school Caroline saw more and more wagons on the Territorial Road. It seemed as if the whole country was moving west. For many folks, like Yorkers, Wisconsin *was* west. But for others, like the Atwoods, there were the open prairies to explore. There was much talk of the rich land in the Kansas Territory. And many were still flooding to California and Oregon for gold.

One day, after they passed several wagons on the way home from school, Eliza suddenly asked Miss May, "Will you be going west too?"

Miss May did not answer right away, and Caroline glanced quickly up into her face.

Caroline had been so happy to have the teacher for another term, she had not wanted to think about what would happen when the term was up.

"As a matter of fact, I have recently come to a decision," Miss May said slowly. She glanced at Caroline. "I thought I would wait to tell you until nearer the end of the term, but since you have asked, I will tell you now."

Caroline studied the muddy road as they continued to walk slowly along. She knew instantly from Miss May's look and tone that the news was not good.

"A few weeks ago I received a letter from my brother, William," Miss May continued. "It seems that he has at last given up his dreams of gold. He has started a school for the children of miners, and he has asked me to join him."

"In California?" Martha cried.

"Yes," Miss May answered.

"But don't you like it here?" Eliza asked.

"Yes, I do," Miss May replied. "But I feel in my heart that I am needed at my brother's side. William says there are very few teachers where he is."

"But there are very few teachers here!" Caroline exclaimed, and right away she felt ashamed. It was childish to speak out so heatedly, and to contradict Miss May's reasons for going. She felt her cheeks burn with embarrassment.

"It will be difficult for me to leave here, now that I have become so fond of you all." Miss May's voice was gentle. "But Mr. Kellogg assures me that it will not be difficult to find a teacher now, because there are so many new settlers."

For the rest of the way home through the woods, Caroline was quiet. It was not fair that Miss May had come into their lives to stay such a short time.

That night at supper they talked of Miss May's journey. Mother and Pa already knew of her decision. The boys did not seem sad at all. They were more interested in how Miss May was going to get to California.

"You'll be going 'round the Horn?" Henry asked. His eyes burned with the same fire they always held when anyone spoke of gold or travel. "Going 'round the Horn" meant taking a ship all the way around the continent of South America, the tip of which looked like a great horn.

"Yes," Miss May replied. "I will travel to Prairie du Chien and then take a steamer down the Mississippi River to New Orleans. I've been told that ships are departing weekly there for San Francisco."

Mother shook her head. "Are you quite sure you wish to go, Patience? It will be many months before you see your brother. And the travel will surely be rough at times."

"I know it will not always be easy, but I am looking forward to the challenge," Miss May replied. "I thank you for your concern, however. And for the generosity and affection you have shown me over the past few months."

That evening before bed Caroline sharpened her quill and wrote in her day journal,

April 2, 1852
  On this day our Miss May has decided to leave us. I will miss her a great deal.

Caroline wanted to write more, but somehow she could not make herself put down her feelings. Suddenly nothing seemed right. Especially not the quill pen in her hand. She was tired of sharpening it and still not being able to get as fine a point as she would have liked. She looked through the few pages she had filled so far and wished her penmanship could be neater.

For the rest of the week Caroline could not shake her melancholy mood. It felt as if she were moving inside a great fog—the kind of fog that sometimes sat heavy in the clearing on rainy mornings. She went about her lessons and helped Miss May before and after school as usual, but she did not smile very much, and she did not talk freely with Miss May as she had always done. She knew she was being childish, but she could not help it.

On Saturday when Miss May offered to help

her look for eggs, Caroline almost said no, but she knew she could never be that rude, especially to Miss May. Together they walked along the edge of the clearing. Caroline found five eggs before she summoned the courage to say what had been on her mind all week.

"I wish you were not going," she said in a low voice. "We will never have a teacher like you again."

"I am glad I have been able to help you in your studies, Caroline. It means a great deal to me that you have enjoyed school so much," Miss May said.

"Oh, I have!" Caroline exclaimed. "I have enjoyed every single day."

"I know my decision to leave disappoints you," Miss May continued gently. "But you must understand that it has been years since I have seen my brother. I do long for a reunion."

Now Caroline felt terrible. How could she be so selfish? Miss May wanted to be with her own family, and of course that was as it should be. Caroline tried to imagine what it would be like to be separated for years from any of her brothers or sisters. It made her heart ache just to think about it.

Caroline wanted to apologize for the way she had been acting over the past few days, but something still held her back. She supposed it was pride, which was a sin. "Pride goeth before a fall," Mother always said.

"Is your brother older than you are?" Caroline asked instead.

"Yes he is," Miss May said, and then she smiled. "But he can be very foolish. Sometimes I feel that I am the one who must look after him, rather than the other way around."

Caroline smiled at this. "I know what you mean. Sometimes it seems as if I am older than Henry, because he can do such silly things." As her own words sank in, she knew she must speak. "I can be very silly as well," she said. "I am sorry. I was angry that you were leaving."

Miss May did not say anything. She reached out and squeezed Caroline's hand, then smiled her warmest smile. "Now, I will expect you to write to me about the goings-on here. I wish to know how your studies are progressing. I will certainly write to you about my journey and about California once I am there."

"You will write to me?" Caroline asked excitedly. The family received letters, of course, but Caroline had never had a letter that was addressed just to her.

"Yes, but you must promise to write me back," Miss May said.

"Oh, I promise," Caroline breathed. Suddenly her heart felt lighter. As they walked back to the house with their basket full of eggs, Caroline felt that she could speak freely to Miss May once more. "Eliza thought you might stay here and find someone to marry," she said.

"Ah!" Miss May laughed. "But if I married, I would have to give up teaching, and I am afraid I am not prepared to do that just yet. I feel that teaching is my calling, Caroline."

"I would like it to be my calling as well," Caroline said in a solemn voice.

"You are still young, Caroline, to make such a

decision." Miss May smiled. "But I believe you will achieve anything you put your mind to."

Caroline's heart swelled to hear Miss May say this.

Now that she had accepted that Miss May was truly leaving, Caroline tried to make each day last. But she could not make time stop altogether, and soon the school term came to an end.

On the last day the scholars gathered together at Miss May's desk to present her with a gift.

"This is so you will not forget us," Maddy Jayson said. She had been elected to speak, since she was the oldest scholar and since they had purchased the gift at her father's store.

The gift was a pretty little wooden box with a clever lid that slid open on tiny grooves. On the top of the lid Mr. Jayson had engraved the words "CONCORD SCHOOL, 1851–1852."

Miss May's face glowed as she gazed at the box. "I will remember each and every one of you," she said, dabbing at the corners of her eyes with her handkerchief.

After that they walked home. Caroline knew it was the last time she would be strolling with Miss May through the woods. As she looked around at the new green leaves fluttering over-head, Caroline thought of the books Miss May had brought with her, books filled with words about long-lost love and times gone by. Miss May had said that the books made her feel at home no matter where she was, and she had told Caroline that writing in her day journal made her feel that events in the past would always be fresh and vivid. Miss May believed that words were powerful, and suddenly Caroline knew this to be true. The people and places Mr. Longfellow had written about in *Evangeline* were gone, but they lived on in his verse. These same woods Caroline had come to know so well were changing each day as more settlers came and cleared the land. Caroline herself was changing. She knew she was growing up, and she wondered if the words she wrote in her day journal would make things any easier.

That evening the mood was solemn inside

the little house. Caroline knew they were all as sad as she was to see Miss May leave, especially Martha, who had come to enjoy school with Miss May teaching. Supper was eaten quietly, and then Miss May retired early to pack her trunks.

In the morning Caroline helped Mother cook a special breakfast. There were Mother's wonderful, fluffy hotcakes, with plenty of fresh butter and maple sugar to drizzle over them. There was fried salt pork and applesauce and fresh, cold milk. After breakfast Caroline helped Mother pack a dinner for Miss May.

"Who knows when you will eat your next meal?" Mother said.

"I know it will be some time before I eat as well as I have eaten here," Miss May replied.

After the dishes had been wiped and put away, Miss May said that she had gifts for them all.

For the boys Miss May had carefully copied on a piece of paper the poem they had liked so much, "The Raven" by Edgar Allan Poe.

To Martha and Eliza she gave the latest copy of *Godey's*, and to Pa she gave a copy of a new newspaper friends had sent her from New York. It was called *The New York Daily Times*.

"This will give me some idea of the goings-on back east, I reckon," Pa said.

To Mother Miss May gave two of the clever safety pins she had shown them when she had first arrived.

"Why, this is too much," Mother exclaimed, but Miss May insisted that it was nothing compared to all that they had given her over the past months.

At last it was Caroline's turn. Miss May handed her an oddly shaped package wrapped in brown paper. When Caroline opened it, she could not believe her eyes. It was Miss May's elegant pearl-handled pen.

"Perhaps now you will find it easier to write in your day journal," Miss May said, smiling down at Caroline fondly.

"Oh, thank you!" Caroline exclaimed, and then she rushed to Miss May and gave her a great hug. "I will miss you," she whispered.

"I will miss you, too," Miss May said, leaning down and planting a kiss on Caroline's forehead.

Caroline watched as Miss May embraced Mother and Martha and Eliza. Then she shook hands with Pa and the boys. Joseph and Henry took Miss May's trunks out of the house and lifted them into the wagon. Then Pa helped Miss May onto the wagon seat. Pa would drive her to Mr. Kellogg's inn, where she would wait for the stagecoach to take her first to Madison, and then on to Prairie du Chien.

Caroline stood beside Martha and Eliza, watching the wagon roll away down the wagon path. Miss May turned once and waved, and then she was gone, swallowed up in the green of the woods.

Caroline promised herself she would not cry, but she went about her Saturday chores with a heavy heart. She helped Mother with the baking, and she saw to the chickens and geese. Late in the afternoon Henry asked if she would mind fetching the cows for him, because one of the hogs was missing, so Caroline called for Wolf, and together they headed for the river.

As she walked, Caroline breathed in the scent of spring. The trees were budding and the bluebells and daffodils had bloomed along the mossy forest floor. The newly green grasses were alive with baby rabbits and squirrels and chipmunks. The air was filled with the merry twitter of songbirds, and as she drew closer to the river, there was the *rush rush* of the swollen river as it flowed along.

Suddenly there was another sound coming through the trees. It was a wonderfully haunting melody, and it did not startle Caroline as it had done when she had first heard it. She knew it was not the trees singing but a honey-colored fiddle. Charlie was not playing the thrush's song, as he had done months before. He was playing an oddly familiar tune. As she came closer, Caroline began to recall the words:

> *Oh Shenandoah, I long to hear you.*
> *Way hey, you rolling river.*
> *Oh Shenandoah, I long to hear you.*

Away, we're bound away
'Cross the wide Missouri.

When Caroline reached the clearing, she found Charlie concentrating on the music he was playing. He did not see her until Wolf gave a little yip, and then he put his fiddle down and grinned.

"Caught me practicing again," he said.

"I like that song," Caroline said. "It's the one the fiddler played that night at the fair."

"That's right," Charlie said. "I like it too. I was just trying to work out the notes. I think I almost have it."

"It sounds like you do," Caroline said. "I mean, what I heard sounded good."

"Thank you kindly," Charlie said.

They were quiet for a little while, watching Wolf sniff along the water's edge.

"How did you get across?" Caroline asked Charlie. "The river's higher than I've ever seen it."

"Aw, this is not such a hard river to wade through," Charlie said. He picked up a rock and skipped it across the water. "It's a tiny thing compared to the rivers they talk about in that song. The Shenandoah or the Missouri."

"Miss May will be traveling down the Mississippi soon," Caroline said.

"Yep, that's another fine river. That teacher's got a lot of pluck to do something like that," Charlie said admiringly. "I wouldn't mind tagging along if I could. I plan to go west when I'm older."

"You're just like Henry," Caroline said. She looked at Charlie, and then she looked at the river. She thought of all the wagons moving along the Territorial Road, of Henry's and Charlie's urge to go west, of Miss May's need to travel so far from home. She wondered why it was that others always wanted to go to new places, when she was content to have a home here in the woods, not far from this rolling river.

Lost in thought, Caroline did not notice that

Charlie had begun playing again until he was singing a verse she had forgotten:

"*Farewell, my dear, I'm bound to leave you.*
Way hey, you rolling river.
Oh, Shenandoah, I'll not deceive you.
Away, we're bound away
'Cross the wide Missouri."

Come Home to Little House

The **MARTHA** *Years*
By Melissa Wiley
Illustrated by Renée Graef

The **CHARLOTTE** *Years*
By Melissa Wiley
Illustrated by Dan Andreasen

The **CAROLINE** *Years*
By Maria D. Wilkes
Illustrated by Dan Andreasen

The **LAURA** *Years*
By Laura Ingalls Wilder
Illustrated by Garth Williams

LITTLE HOUSE IN THE BIG WOODS

LITTLE HOUSE ON THE PRAIRIE

FARMER BOY

ON THE BANKS OF PLUM CREEK

BY THE SHORES OF SILVER LAKE

THE LONG WINTER

LITTLE TOWN ON THE PRAIRIE

THESE HAPPY GOLDEN YEARS

THE FIRST FOUR YEARS

The ROSE *Years*
By Roger Lea MacBride
Illustrated by Dan Andreasen
& David Gilleece